Posse Guns

POSSE GUNS

A WESTERN SEXTET

PETER DAWSON

FIVE STAR
A part of Gale, Cengage Learning

Detroit • New York • San Francisco • New Haven, Conn • Waterville, Maine • London

GALE
CENGAGE Learning

LIBRARY OF CONGRESS CATALOGING-IN-PUBLICATION DATA

Dawson, Peter, 1907–1957.
    Posse guns : a western sextet / by Peter Dawson. — 1st ed.
      p. cm.
    ISBN-13: 978-1-59414-688-6 (alk. paper)
    ISBN-10: 1-59414-688-8 (alk. paper)
    I. Title.
PS3507.A848P67 2008
813'.54—dc22   2008016367

First Edition. First Printing: August 2008.
Published in 2008 in conjunction with Golden West Literary Agency.

CONTENTS

★ ★ ★ ★ ★

OUTCAST DEPUTY

★ ★ ★ ★ ★

This story under the title "An Outcast Deputy's Brand of Luck" was submitted by Jon Glidden's agent to *Complete Western Book Magazine* shortly after it was finished. It was sold on November 3, 1940 and the author was paid $108. The title was changed by editor Ward Marshal to "Land-Grabber, I'll Be Back with Guns!" when it appeared in the issue dated March, 1941. For its first book appearance the author's original title has been shortened.

I

The cabin had lost its air of disuse. New yellow pine shakes unevenly splotched the gray, tinder-dry slant of its roof, and along its sides showed an occasional fresh slab with the bark still brown and yellow. The wagon shed out back gave evidence of the same neat hand, while the lean-to near the corral was new and staunchly built. And the green carpet of the valley pasture climbed the knoll and made a pleasing yard out front, a yard now orderly where three months ago brush and rusty tin cans had completed the layout's desolate appearance.

Hugh Conner, his tall, flat frame propped indolently against one corner of his cabin, gazed unsmilingly at the two men standing near their ground-haltered ponies thirty feet out in the yard, and said tonelessly: "No one wanted it, so I'm here."

"Someone wants it now." The tallest of the pair growled his words, his belligerence obvious. He was thin almost to gauntness, and on the upper left-hand pocket of the vest beneath his canvas windbreaker showed a sheriff's five-pointed star. His light-colored blue eyes were red-rimmed and dull from too much whiskey. Sheriff Mace Dow didn't command the respect due his badge.

"Who wants it?"

"I've already filed on it," answered Mace Dow's companion. "One of my crew will be up here next week. He's homesteading in my name."

"Why didn't you come to me before you filed, Keyes?"

Wyatt Keyes lifted his thick shoulders in a careless shrug. "You're a squatter, Conner. I didn't think it necessary to consult you."

His sarcasm was biting, eloquent of the man's habitual arrogance. Looking at Keyes now, Hugh Conner wondered at the stubborn will that had brought the man so far in ten years. This last summer Keyes's Key-Bar had calmly bluffed George Baird's Chain Link, the biggest outfit in this country, and made Baird give over ten sections of choice summer graze high in the hills. A legal loophole had made it possible, and with the help of his sheriff—Mace Dow had two years ago been Key-Bar foreman—he'd made it stick. Now he was buying up this valley. Hugh hadn't been surprised at their call this afternoon, for he had heard of Keyes's visits to some of his neighbors above, but it galled him to have to give up something he had made from nothing and with his own hands; every day for three months, since the time he first came to this country, he had worked at his cabin and his fence, believing that it was his home.

"And if I don't get out?"

Keyes and Dow both smiled. "We'll change your mind." As Keyes spoke, he hooked his thumbs significantly in his shell belts within finger spread of the ivory-handled guns, slung low in tooled holsters at his thighs. He was full of confidence, his solid body mirroring a physical strength that backed a strong will.

Hugh Conner got the second hint of the reason for their visit from Mace Dow. The lawman's eyes had clouded over and now the fingers of his right hand clawed and stiffened. So they were here to shoot it out with him.

As his eyes settled on Mace's wrist, knowing that the first sign of the man's draw would be telegraphed plainly, Hugh drawled: "There's an election in town today. Maybe that'll change things."

"Mace will be reëlected sheriff," Keyes answered.

Hugh shook his head. "I reckon not. There's too many decent people in this county to see that happen again."

He saw Mace's wrist muscles bulge, saw that hand move a fraction of an inch. Suddenly, from far out across the pasture, came the strident, wild yelping of a dog. He saw Mace's hand relax and looked up to see both the lawman and Keyes looking out across the valley. Then his glance followed theirs. A dog was bounding in long strides in toward the cabin with a full-grown jack rabbit streaking ahead in twenty-foot leaps; the dog's ears were pointed and his full-throated cry was piercing and high-pitched, showing a wild ancestry.

As Dow and Keyes looked back at Hugh again, too wary to witness the finish of that race, Hugh saw the dog swing close, not fifty yards away. "Excuse me, gents," he drawled, shoving himself out from the wall of the cabin. "There's the calf killer I've been hunting."

Before they could read his intention, his two hands flowed smoothly up from his sides. They moved faster than the eye could follow, and, when they settled at his hips, they rocked into position two Colt .38s. His right-hand gun bucked in his hand, to send a hollow blast ripping out across the valley, then, in one prolonged inferno of sound, five more shots beat out. At the first explosion the dog's steady stride broke and his front legs went limp and he rolled over in a sprawl; five times that furry body jerked from a slug's impact. When sudden silence edged out the far echoes of those shots, Hugh slid his weapons back into leather and said: "Now what were you saying, Keyes?"

Wyatt Keyes's eyes mirrored unfeigned surprise, while Mace Dow's mouth gaped open in sheer astonishment at the gun magic he had witnessed.

Finally Keyes growled: "We'll be back, Conner." He turned. "Let's be goin', Mace." He led the way back to the horses.

Keyes was satisfied with the implications behind his last threat. But Mace Dow wasn't; he reined his pony close in to Hugh and bent down in the saddle to take a parting jibe. "Maybe I ought to look through some of the Reward posters I've been throwin' in that empty drawer of my desk, Conner."

"Maybe you had, Mace. Maybe you'd find your own picture on one of 'em."

Dow's face clouded a brick red as he swung away, wordless. He had seen enough during the past few minutes to make him ride check on his temper.

When they were out of sight in the bend on the trail below, Hugh sighed gustily and took off his Stetson and wiped the sweat out of its band. It had been close, too close, and he was momentarily thankful that these two hadn't driven him to using his guns on them.

I wonder what he knows? he mused, recalling that last remark of the lawman's. But then his concern left him. Mace Dow couldn't know, or he'd have come up here with a warrant. Four months ago Hugh Conner had spent two nights and three days outriding a posse far to the north. A glory hunter had prodded him into using his guns, and a forked sheriff, fearing the influence of the dead man's friends, had turned a deaf ear to Hugh's plea of self-defense. So there had been a jail break, a deputy with a broken jaw—and that hard ride across the state line.

Now, having found this small, unwanted place and taken it for his own, he was being driven out for no reason that he knew. He would have to go; that much was certain, for Keyes wouldn't return without guns to back him the next time. Perhaps he wouldn't even bother to come back. There were a hundred places in the timber above the cabin where a bushwhacker could hide to put a bullet between Hugh's shoulders some morning.

He looked out at the dead dog lying at the border of the pasture. "Thanks, friend," he muttered. "You made up for all the critters you've dragged down in coming along when you did."

He stood there a moment, wondering what would happen if he stayed and fought Keyes. Mace Dow might lose the election today—although that was unlikely, with all Keyes's backing— and a new lawman might recognize his prior rights to the property. But in staying to fight, he was running a risk; someone might be curious about him and do what Dow had threatened— look at the Reward dodgers. And there might be one with his name on it.

No, he'd get out of the country, bury himself in obscurity somewhere south, closer to the border. But before he left, he'd make a play that Keyes and Dow wouldn't forget. He already knew how he was going to do it. It would be a petty, unsatisfying revenge, but he wasn't going to crawl out like a whipped dog.

He went out to the lean-to, intent on the first thing to be done. Out there he drained half a bucket of coal oil from a nearly empty barrel and took it to the house. He rolled his few personal belongings into a blanket, and then sloshed the coal oil liberally over his bunk and along the base of the walls. With one last, regretful look at what had been his home for three months, he flicked alight a match and tossed it into the bunk. A puff of blaze burst outward and climbed the wall, spreading fast.

He fired the lean-to and the wagon shed in the same manner. Ten minutes later, from his saddle on a higher knoll one hundred yards above, he looked down on the layout. Three black pillars of smoke plumed high in the still, crisp air, the flames already showing along the cabin's near wall.

"It'll do."

He wheeled his claybank gelding and rode straight up the valley, toward the low pass to the north that cut between the jagged snow-capped peaks ahead. He'd wait out the rest of the day in the timber above, and tonight, late, he'd ride in to Bull Forks and hunt up Dow and Keyes and name them as the men who fired his place. The election crowd would be there and not many would soon forget his visit.

He was striking into the trees a mile above when his forward glance made out the figure of a rider half hidden beneath the leafless aspens on the trail ahead. Instinctively his right hand fell to his side in a wary gesture, but the next instant he had recognized the rider and his hand came away.

Fay Baird sat her dun pony with a straight-backed, easy grace that always stirred him to admiration. Today she was outfitted in worn, blue Levi's, a cotton shirt open at the throat, and a dark brown buckskin jacket that gave only a hint of her square shoulders and boyish body. Her hair caught the tree-branched pattern of sunlight and took on a coppery sheen he had never before noticed.

As he drew rein twenty feet away, she frowned in mock severity and said: "Aren't you going to speak to me, Hugh?"

Once again he caught the strong flavor of her friendliness, and he knew that his one regret in leaving this country would be losing the promise of these rare moments with her. The Chain Link, her home, was ten miles out from this valley, yet he saw her occasionally in town, and after their first meeting she had been this way, friendly without forwardness, and feeling a measure of the same thing that had attracted him to her.

"You saw me . . . what I did down there?" he queried, wanting to get this over with.

"I did, Hugh. And I saw Keyes and his understrapper ride away. What does it mean?"

"It's Keyes's place now. I'm leavin' as little of it as I can."

"His place? Then he's been to see you, too. Dad and a few

others are wondering why he wants this valley. Are you leaving, Hugh?"

He nodded his answer.

"Without a fight?" Her look turned abruptly serious. "Without a fight, Hugh?"

"It would be one man against his whole outfit . . . and against his lawman. It's not worth a dose of lead poison for me to stay and find out why he wants this place. I'm pulling out."

"But it won't be one man against Keyes. Walt Andrews may win the election today. If he does, things will change."

"He won't win. He can't. But suppose he does? That'll be two against Keyes. Not enough."

"But there's Dad. . . ."

"George Baird fight?" Hugh's sudden laughter was mocking. "I don't think so. Your father lost his chance at Keyes when he pulled off that hill range this summer."

"But I intend to make him fight!" Suddenly the flashing light in her brown eyes quieted before a resigned look. She sighed and lifted her shoulders in a shrug. "Of course, Walt Andrews won't win. I came up here to get these people to go down and vote for him. But it won't help much."

To see her high spirits so weighted down by a lost hope made Hugh Conner wish there was some way he could help her and her friends before he left. He stared unseeingly back at the burning cabin, idly turning over in his mind a thought that had just come to him. Abruptly he turned to face the girl.

"There's a way you can win that election, Fay." His gray eyes were narrow-lidded now and a faint smile played across his aquiline features. "How long will it take you to ride to town?"

"An hour if I hurry."

"Four o'clock. That may be time enough." He lifted a hand and pointed to the billowing smoke cloud spreading out above the tops of the trees. "Can you ride in and tell your father and

Walt Andrews and a few others that you saw Keyes and Dow riding down the valley, and that later you found my place had been fired? Can you put that story across?"

"But it wouldn't be the truth." The shrewd light that had come to her eyes belied the protest.

"It would. You saw Keyes and Dow. Later, you saw my place on fire. You can leave out the rest. Ten minutes after you get that story started, Mace Dow won't get one vote out of ten. It's a way of winning for Walt Andrews. Will you do it?"

She looked at him with a softness in her glance that was a mute plea. "Will you stay, Hugh?"

"What does that have to do with this other?"

"It means you'll be with us fighting Keyes."

"I'll decide that later," he told her. "Right now you've got a job on your hands. Play it right and you'll win. I'll be in town tonight to see how the election turns out."

He leaned across and slapped her dun across the hindquarters to startle the animal into a quick run. As she headed out across the pasture, she turned in the saddle and waved and called back something he didn't catch.

He sat there, watching her, once more feeling that deep regret in losing this friend. He felt better about leaving now; his petty revenge rankled less against his pride, for as it had turned out he was helping the people he would have wanted to help if he'd stayed. And maybe he could do one more thing to help them before he rode away.

II

Room *14* in the Mountain View Hotel had served as Mace Dow's headquarters throughout the day. Four hours ago it had been full to overflowing with a riotous, odorous crowd of drunken voters. Wyatt Keyes's friend, Faro Mike, owner of the Palace Bar, had loaned his best barkeep for the occasion and

16

supplied all the whiskey; Faro Mike expected favors in return, namely that Dow would continue to let him run his place wide open and to keep on using the itinerant faro and poker dealers who ran the crooked tables in his place. The town ordinance requiring saloons to close at midnight, and restricting the play at gaming tables had not been enforced for two years. It was to Faro Mike's advantage to see that it wasn't for another two.

The afternoon didn't turn out the way Keyes and Dow and Faro Mike had planned it. Around 4:00 p.m. they heard the story that was making the rounds—the story that Hugh Conner had been burned out and that they were being blamed for it. Fay Baird, whose word was gospel, had seen Keyes and his sheriff riding away from Hugh's and had gone on to find his buildings a blazing ruin.

The news had worked like magic. Room *14* had emptied first, leaving nothing but a litter of empty bottles and broken glasses, cigarette butts and cigar ash strewn about the floor, and a few drunks asleep in the room's half dozen chairs. 5:00 p.m. had seen Mace Dow's headquarters deserted. And from then on people who hadn't yet voted made no bones about saying which way their ballots were being cast. Walt Andrews was their man, and to hell with Keyes and his crowd!

Now, at 9:00 p.m., three men waited in room *14;* across the street was the unused hall above the saddle shop where the election judges were counting the votes, and below in the street waited an eager, boisterous crowd. Mace Dow sat with his ungainly frame slumped in a deep leather chair, his eyes bleary from too much whiskey, his speech thick as he muttered: "Half a dozen gents could go across and get those ballots. Burn 'em. And if they called a new election, we'd make sure this time."

Keyes sat with one leg thrown over the corner of a rickety table. He surveyed his lawman with a cold, disgusted stare. "We don't do things that way from now on, Mace. There's plenty of time." He shifted his glance from Dow to the third occupant of the room, a tallish man outfitted in a tight-fitting serge suit and a derby hat, who paced restlessly back and forth in front of the window, where a drawn blind cut off the view of the street and the closed window muffled the mutterings of the crowd below.

"Nothing to worry about, Summers," Keyes said softly, an easy smile playing across his square features. "The way the election goes doesn't have anything to do with our proposition. You might as well go to your room and turn in."

The stranger, Summers, shook his head emphatically and met Keyes's smile with a quality of stoniness in his eyes that baffled any attempt at heartiness. "I don't like it," he snapped, and it was plain that he was a willful man. "I don't like the smell of the whole thing."

"Maybe you'd like to pull out of the deal."

"Don't be a damn' fool!" Summers blazed, unimpressed. "I've bought myself into this and I'll play the hand out. But I hate to see a perfect layout blasted by a childish move. Why did you do it?"

"Once again, we didn't burn Conner's place." Keyes breathed, his mouth a thin, tight line at his sudden rise of temper. "I tell you it's a frame-up."

"It'll make it harder. You'll have a tough job doing this in three weeks. That's when Sierra Central expects my report on the right of way and I'd better show up with the deeds to all that valley property."

"Since when does a railroad have to settle a matter of right of way in three weeks?"

Summers hid his impatience behind a cloak of suavity, his belligerence abruptly giving away before a studied, biting sarcasm.

"Once again, Keyes, here are the reasons. Fifty miles west there's another low pass through these hills. We took out an option on the land down there before we knew about this. That option expires in three weeks. The Denver and Southern are ready to take up that option, if we release it. They'll build through there. Now, if we can buy up this valley of yours and lay steel through the pass above, well and good. It's better than the other, and means we'll get through ahead of the Denver and Southern. But if we don't get this valley inside of three weeks, we've got to take the other, whether we like it or not. And you're out."

"And you're out!"

"And I'm out. But get this, Keyes. Before I'm out, I'll go to those valley ranchers myself and offer them the full amount, two hundred a section. My future depends on keeping my job with Sierra Central."

"Your future depends on me," Keyes corrected.

For a long, tense moment the two men eyed each other with unveiled hostility. Finally Summers shrugged, smiled, and said: "What the hell are we rowing about? This will go through, like you say. You've taken out options on most of the valley and bought a few outfits at twenty and thirty a section. The deal still holds, Keyes. You get a hundred a section for the whole works. I take my cut of fifty and turn back fifty to the railroad. They'll make me a director for saving them the money."

"I wonder," Keyes mused brutally. "I wonder if you'll turn that fifty back to Sierra Central."

"That's something you'll never know, Keyes. And, in case you get any wild ideas, there's a signed and sealed statement in my office safe that'll take care of you if anything happens to me."

"Forget it," Keyes said, trying to smooth over his tone but making poor effort. "Why would I cut the bottom out of my own pocketbook?"

"Why would you cut your own throat, you mean. Together,

we can go a long way. But if you. . . ."

He bit off his words, all at once listening to the undertone of the crowd outside lift to a pulsing roar. Keyes came down off the table, crossed the room to turn down the lamp on the ornamental fireplace, and then went to the window. Mace got up out of his chair and followed, leaning heavily against Summers as the shade went up and Keyes raised the window.

A blast of sound filled the room. The street below was packed with shouting people whose faces were upturned to where a man stood at a lighted window of the room above the saddle shop. Keyes and his companions could see into the room across there, could see the litter of paper that strewed the floor under the long table where the judges had been counting the ballots.

The shouting below died slowly. A few jeers of "Down with Dow!" and "Get rid of Keyes's understrapper!" rang out, and then there was quiet, a silence that flowed out in waves along the half-lighted street to the crowds in front of the saloons.

The election judge in the window across the street cleared his throat, and the sound plainly shuttled across the interval to Keyes and his companion. Then came the words: "Ladies and gentlemen. The count has been totaled and certified by the Committee on Elections. For Mace Dow, eight hundred and twenty-two votes. For Walter Andrews, one thousand four hundred. . . ."

From there on his rising words were lost in a roar that muffled even the unruly blast of a six-gun someone fired farther down the street. The crowd went wild, shouting madly; hats were thrown in the air and the flat, hollow explosions of other guns joined the first. The fringes of the crowd melted to the awninged walks as men headed for the town's saloons to celebrate Walt Andrews's victory. Twenty or thirty people mounted the hotel steps below, obviously in search of the new sheriff.

Mace Dow reached over Keyes's shoulder and slammed the

window shut and turned and headed for the door to the hall.

"Where to, Mace?" Keyes called out, seeing his lawman's back disappearing into the dimly lit hallway.

"Down to Mike's," was Dow's surly answer. "And if any jasper tries to rub it in on me, Walt Andrews can damn' well make me his first arrest!"

The door slammed with a violence that shook the one faded picture on the room's side wall.

Summers's brows gathered in a studied frown as he gazed at the closed door. "Sometimes I don't understand you, Keyes. Take Dow, for instance. He's. . . ."

"I know. Maybe I'm about through with Mace."

III

From the narrow alleyway between the two stores across from the hotel, Hugh Conner witnessed the breaking up of the crowd, saw Mace Dow walk, spraddle-legged, down the steps, and shove his way roughly along the walk toward Faro Mike's. Hugh waited two minutes longer, hoping to see Keyes follow Mace.

He smiled and reached down to loosen his guns carefully in their holsters. Then, pulling his Stetson low over his eyes, he went on down the walk in the same direction Mace had taken.

He took his time about it, so that it was ten minutes before he crossed the street and shouldered through the bat-wings of the Palace. Only a dozen men stood at the bar, the tables were nearly deserted, a few percentage girls spotted here and there among the drinkers. The other saloons were getting the play tonight, for Faro Mike had placed his bets on the wrong horse in this race and this was the pay-off.

Hugh's glance shuttled quickly over the scene before him. Most of these men were Key-Bar riders and they took their whiskey in silence, still awed by the turn of events none of them had expected. The lamps glowed dully from their brackets on the ceiling and the walls, penetrating the thick smoke haze to give the room a blue, foggy look.

Hugh smiled thinly. If it had been arranged especially for his purpose, things couldn't have been nicer. Mace Dow stood bellied to the bar, talking with Faro Mike over the counter. Mike was a slick-haired, chinless little man outfitted in a black coat and tie and a pink shirt that matched his pale skin. Just now his beady eyes glanced toward the swing doors and he caught sight of Hugh and spoke quickly to Mace.

The ex-sheriff turned slowly, propped his elbows on the bar, and faced Hugh. His gesture was a signal for silence. Others had seen, and with one or two exceptions they were Wyatt Keyes's friends and had no love for Hugh.

Across the hush of the room, Mace said: "Look who's here."

Faro Mike put in his word: "Get out, Conner! Get out before I have you thrown out!" He nodded significantly to three men standing at the end of the bar, men whose breadth of shoulder and thick chests and arms named them for what they were, Mike's bouncers.

"I don't think I will," Hugh drawled. "Mike, I'm goin' to take your place apart. Mace, I'm goin' to take you apart."

On the heel of his words he let his right hand flow up smoothly and palm out a heavy Colt. Mace had seen the beginning of that move and sent his two hands stabbing down at his guns. But Hugh's weapon suddenly thundered into the silence, and a chip flew from the molding of Mike's shiny bar less than half an inch from Mace's downswinging right wrist. He took his hands from his sides as though someone had prodded him in the back with a loaded shotgun.

To one side of Mace Dow, behind him and at the rear wall, Hugh saw a man he recognized as Shorty Crowe of the Key-Bar edge cautiously behind his neighbor. Hugh swung his Colt around and thumbed a shot that slapped into the weathered board alongside Shorty's hat brim. The man in front threw himself flat on his face, exposing Shorty with his hand closed on his gun butt. He let go of the handle of his weapon as though it had suddenly become a white-hot iron, calling out stridently: "Lay off, Conner! Swing your cutter away!"

Hugh sauntered across until he stood six feet in front of Mace. "Had enough, lawman?"

Mace glared, but made no answer, speechless in his humiliation. Abruptly Hugh reached out with his left hand and took hold of the sheriff's badge on Mace's shirt pocket and brought his hand down in a sudden motion that ripped the other's shirt wide open. "Your turn's over, Mace. Go back to cow nursing."

At the limits of his vision Hugh saw Faro Mike make a stealthy move of one hand beneath the bar. Tossing the sheriff's badge on the bar top, he reached quickly for a tin tray used by the barkeeps for serving drinks to the tables; he took it by its rim and with a flick of the wrist sailed it into the mirror behind Mike. It whirled true, knocking down a row of bottles and a mound of half a hundred glasses before it crashed into the mirror.

Mike straightened from his crouch and raised his arm to protect himself from the flying glass, knocking a double-barreled shotgun from its hangers under the bar. Hugh laughed mirthlessly. "Go ahead, Mike, pick it up!"

The *crack* of the swing-door hinges up front cut in on Hugh's words. He jerked his head around in time to see Walt Andrews step through the doors and stop, his brown eyes wide in amazement. Andrews was seeing a crowd of men with upthrust hands standing quietly along the far wall, the bar mirror wrecked, and the place filling with the stench of spilled whiskey, Mace Dow with his torn shirt, and Hugh Conner with a Colt held steadily in his hand, leaning carelessly back against the bar as though unmindful of the twenty men who faced him.

Bull Forks' new sheriff tried not to smile, yet his inner amusement was betrayed in the warm light that crept into his brown eyes. He said: "Put up your gun and come along with me, Hugh."

In answer he got a brief shake of the head. Hugh moved the snout of his weapon two inches, until it covered the lawman. "Not tonight, Sheriff. Not any other night. I'm leaving the country." He reached around and picked up the badge he had torn from Mace Dow's shirt and tossed it across so that it lit at Andrews's feet. "Pin it on, Sheriff. I'm wishin' you luck with it."

Walt Andrews looked down at the badge. He didn't pick it up. Instead, he reached into a back pocket of his Levi's, slowly, so that Hugh wouldn't misunderstand the move. He brought his hand out and tossed something back at Hugh—an object that flashed as it reflected the light of the hanging lamps overhead and lit with a ringing sound at Hugh's feet. Hugh looked down, saw a five-pointed star with *Deputy Sheriff* lettered across its face.

"Pin it on, Hugh. Maybe between us we can make our own brand of luck." Then, without waiting for Hugh to answer, Andrews's face went serious again and he looked across at Faro Mike and said: "This place is to be closed at midnight tonight, and every night from now on, Mike. My deputy here will be around to see to it. Hugh, if this place is open at one minute past twelve, wreck it like you wanted. Come over to my office and I'll swear you in."

IV

Last night Hugh had listened to Walt Andrews with suspicion. He'd gone out of the Palace with Bull Forks' new sheriff and down to the jail, still thinking that, before the night was over, he'd go to the deserted lean-to in the alley where his claybank was hidden and climb into the saddle and ride away.

But Andrews was an honest man and showed it. "The girl told me about it, Hugh. George Baird's girl. I reckon I owe the two of you a heap more than I can ever pay back. But I can try and I'm starting now. I need a good deputy and you look like the right man . . . just like Fay Baird said you would. Here, lift your right hand and repeat these words after me. . . ."

This morning, having had a few hours' sleep at the hotel after a night spent mainly in quieting drunks too full of election-day whiskey, Hugh Conner was again a little awed at the turn of events. Instead of being on his way to hide from the law, he was wearing a law badge and would someday probably read a Reward dodger with his own name on it. He didn't have to ask himself what had made him take Andrews's offer; it was Kay Baird, the knowledge that she needed him. She had found Walt Andrews a deputy.

Turning in at the jail office walk, Hugh saw a buckboard at the hitch rail in front. The horses were jaw-branded Chain Link. He hesitated about going in, thinking that the girl might be in there with Andrews. Just then the sheriff opened the door and called out: "Hugh, you're needed in here!"

George Baird was Andrews's only visitor. He nodded a greeting to Hugh, and the sheriff said: "George has brought me some news, Hugh. You'd better hear it."

"You tell him, Walt," Baird said. The Chain Link owner was a man of Andrews's generation, turning fifty, massive and with a deep, powerful voice and outfitted exactly like the men who worked for him—Levi's, cotton shirt, buffalo coat, worn boots, and a faded gray Stetson. He wore no guns. Hugh knew about that—Baird's hatred of guns—and couldn't understand it. Baird had lived by those guns twenty years ago, when they had helped him carve his small empire out of this wild country. But like many successful men, George Baird argued against the very things that had brought him his success; he had put his guns away years ago, claiming that a man who couldn't get what he wanted by peaceable means in these quiet days was nothing better than an outlaw. The day for guns was past. Perhaps this philosophy was his reason for backing down to Wyatt Keyes last summer and losing ten sections of his choice range.

Just now Walt Andrews cleared his throat and told Hugh: "We've all been wondering what Keyes wanted of that valley up your way, Hugh. The man's got more room than he needs and it seemed damned unreasonable to drive out a bunch of small ranchers and squatters just to fence in more. This morning George heard something that may tell us."

"Now don't get me wrong, Walt," Baird hastened to interrupt. "I don't say it means a thing. I don't want to start any hard feelings with Wyatt Keyes."

Andrews frowned. "If anyone starts anything with Keyes, it'll be me or Hugh. George, damn it, when are you going to rear onto your hind legs and stand up for your rights?"

"That has nothing to do with this, Walt. Suppose you tell Conner what you started to."

Andrews checked his rise of temper and turned to Hugh again. "George stayed at the hotel last night. This morning, coming down to breakfast, he saw Keyes talking at the desk with a stranger, a city man. They hadn't heard him come down the stairs, and, as George walked past the desk, he heard this stranger tell Keyes . . . 'Get up there today and find out for sure. And remember, don't send Mace Dow. You're through with him or I'm through.' Now what do you make of that, Hugh?"

"A stranger?" Hugh mused. "Telling Keyes he was through with Mace?" He shrugged. "I can't make anything of it."

"I can," the lawman said. "I think this jasper was telling Keyes not to send Mace up the valley to dicker with those people who won't sell to Keyes. Something's going on around here we ought to know about, Hugh. Suppose you loaf around the hotel today and see what you can pick up on that stranger. See where he's from, what he's doing, who he works for. There won't be much else doing day after election."

Hugh turned toward the door.

"Another thing, Conner," Baird said. "I saw Keyes later and he swears he didn't fire your place yesterday."

Hugh grinned broadly. "Ask the sheriff about that." He left the office.

Baird looked at his friend. "Well, Walt?"

Andrews's face had taken on a tide of deeper color. "Hell, George, you might as well know. Hugh fired his own place. Fay saw him do it from where she was watching up above his pasture. They cooked up this yarn between 'em, after Keyes and Dow had made a try at kicking Hugh off his place. It's what put me in office."

"You mean Fay lied to me?"

"She didn't. She told the truth . . . but just enough to suit her."

"But . . ."—Baird was choked with indignation—"why would she deceive me? Why would she . . . ?"

"Because she knows you, George. Because she knew you'd spoil her play. Because she wants to get you riled up so you'll start packin' your guns again and use 'em on Keyes the next time he tramples on you. Hell, George, there was a time when you'd spit in a range bull's eye if he looked sideways at you. I'd like to see you in the same frame of mind again. Don't think Keyes is through with you. In five more years he aims to take over your place as one of his line camps, the way things are going."

Baird stood up, his lips pressed so tightly together that they had turned white. "I never thought I'd hear that sort of talk from you, Walt."

"You'll hear that and plenty more," Andrews stubbornly insisted. "And when you're at home, Fay is going to ride you double-rigged. George, Wyatt Keyes has something up his sleeve. When he gets ready to show his hand, I'll need every friend I've got. And when that time comes, I aim to see you swinging a pair of cutters at your hips. Now, if you're sore, go outside and cool off. I've spoken my piece and I feel a lot better for it."

Baird stomped out of the office, his massive body squarely erect, his chin set stubbornly. Walt Andrews chuckled as the door slammed. Maybe he'd given his friend too big a bite to chew all at once. *But he can handle it,* he growled to himself. *George hasn't got store teeth, and, when he swallows that piece, he may find he's got some guts to digest it.*

V

Gerald P. Summers was a cautious man. Instead of loafing in the lobby throughout the day, he kept to his room, out of sight. He didn't welcome this prolonged stay in Bull Forks, cooped up in a hotel room, but in the past he had put himself to even greater discomfort for less money and it had taught him patience. Tonight, late probably, Wyatt Keyes would be in with definite word of the progress he had made in the valley during the day. Tomorrow noon Summers would be on his way to Denver with a full report for the directors. Looking forward to that meeting, he permitted himself a satisfied smile at the thought that soon, very soon, he would be one of them. The Sierra Central was progressive enough to reward a man's efforts.

He ate his noon meal in a corner of the nearly deserted dining room, knowing that he could get better food at any one of the three lunch rooms on down the street, but not wanting to run the risk of making himself too conspicuous. As he started back to his room, he had a thought that made him turn and go over to the desk. He borrowed a sheet of paper from the clerk and stood there, writing for a full minute. Then he folded the paper, went upstairs and got his hat, and came down and went out the front door.

He walked unhurriedly to the first corner, turned down a side street, and in about one hundred yards crossed the railroad tracks and turned in at the station. Inside, he said to the man behind the wicket—"Get this off right away."—and tossed two silver dollars onto the counter. He got his change and went straight back to his room at the hotel to read a three-day-old Denver paper.

Hugh followed him. He waited for five minutes before he crossed the rutted street and went into the station. He found the station agent in his cubbyhole office, straightening some papers on the desk beside his telegraph key. The hand phone to the instrument hung at his neck; he was getting ready to send a message.

He turned at Hugh's entrance, grinned broadly, and said: "They tell me you're doin' over the Palace, Conner."

Hugh smiled and breathed a little hard, as though he had been running. "It's getting so a gent can't have any more fun in this town." Then: "I'm in time, I see. You haven't sent it yet?"

"Sent what?"

"That message my friend just brought in. He wanted to change a word or two. He was busy, so I offered to come down here for him."

As Hugh spoke, a flicker of suspicion edged into the agent's glance. But when the explanation was complete, he reached around and took a sheet of paper from beside his instrument and pushed it through the wicket. "Here it is. I haven't even read it yet. You got a pencil?"

Hugh shook his head, and the agent reached up for a pencil behind his ear and gave it to Hugh.

The message read:

S.M. Hornblow, President
Sierra Central Railroad Offices,
Hulbert and Clark Streets,
Denver, Colorado
Business to be concluded tonight. Everything looks favorable for delivery of deeds in three weeks' time. Will give full report at meeting Saturday.

G.P. Summers

Hugh scratched out the word *Saturday* and wrote *Saturday* above it, handing it back through the wicket again along with the pencil. "Much obliged. Hurry and get it off."

As he turned away, the agent looked down at the message and asked: "Is the road buyin' some property?"

Hugh shrugged. "As near as I can make out, they're running a spur up from Colgate to that coal mine beyond Cow Creek. They're having a little trouble getting a right of way. Don't mention it, though."

"Not me."

Hugh took his time about getting back to the sheriff's office, wanting to digest the facts he had gathered. Summers's wire was easily readable along with the few facts he already knew. It was plain that Summers and Keyes were working together to get control of the valley, probably for a right of way. The Sierra Central's main line came through Bull Forks, had been put through four years ago, and had been unprofitable from many standpoints. Traffic to the West was light, and three bad years had even seen the ranchers shipping little beef to the East. But over the mountains, to the north, lay a rich, protected valley that ran along the jagged peaks of the Saw Tooth range for nearly one hundred miles. As yet no railroad had touched it, chiefly because the cost of running a line over the mountains had so far been prohibitive.

But Hugh knew now that the Sierra Central had found a way—through the pass that lay at the head of the valley where he had lived these past few months. What was Keyes getting out of it all? He thought he knew. Summers and Keyes were in together to get the land cheaply. And Keyes was being paid for his work.

Paid lots, or he wouldn't be in it, Hugh mused. Then he remembered the telegram, its veiling of the truth, and the logical answer came to him, that somehow G. P. Summers—who was registered at the hotel as H. Riley of Carson, Nevada—was also in this for money. *If he can buy up land for a song, he'll have a nice piece of change left over.*

The thing was agonizingly simple, so simple that he hesitated in believing that he had discovered the truth. He hurried his steps a little, wanting to tell Andrews what he had learned. Between them they should be able to think this out.

VI

It was the small, six-section outfit at the head of the valley that presented the biggest problem. Keyes had known it from the first—that old Ben White would be a hard nut to crack. And now, as he sat on White's porch and looked across at the aging man sitting in a chair at the other end of the door, he was somehow amused to think that such a small stumbling block threatened the whole scheme he and Summers had so carefully mapped out.

"You say you're comfortable here, that you don't need money, that you won't sell. What would you say to a hundred dollars a section for movin' out if I'd give you six sections of my best grass in exchange? The money would be clear profit and you'd

31

be down out of the winter."

White leaned forward in his chair, took a bit-chewed pipe from his mouth, and spat out across the rail, running the back of his hand beneath his corn-silk mustache as he settled back in his seat again. "Keyes, I've set up here for ten years watchin' you Bull Forks ranchers fight it out among yourselves. I've saved a little, had a lot of satisfaction out of bein' where I was. I hear tell how Walt Andrews won the election yesterday. That's the way it ought to be. You've been ridin' too wide and too high to suit me. You can't give a good reason for wantin' this place, which looks queer. If you gave me a gold-plated saddle and the finest six sections of your range, I wouldn't stir for a thousand a section. I think you're tryin' to pull a forked deal here. You can get out any time you feel like it."

Without a further word, White got up from his chair and stalked inside his house. He had spoken with an old man's tempered bitterness, in a passionless statement-of-fact manner that was eloquently contemptuous of Keyes. He left Keyes with a fevered flush suffusing the Key-Bar owner's face and neck, and a speechless anger keeping him rooted in his chair. Alone on the porch, in the full view of the three riders who had come up here with him and were waiting at the far limits of the hard-packed yard, Keyes felt like a fool.

He got up finally, sauntered off the steps, and walked over to his horse, trying to hide the rage that had taken hold of him. "We'll ride," he said curtly, and went up into the saddle. He led his men two miles down the valley, then, without any announcement of his intention, he cut off across a park-like meadow and took to a little used trail that wound up and over a hummock through the cedars. On the far side, he drew rein beside the pool of a clear-watered spring and climbed down out of the saddle and announced briefly: "We stay here till after dark."

Dusk came in less than an hour. He silently watched his men

build a fire and cook a meal, running over in his mind the things he had done so far to help Summers. Today he had jolted Mace by telling him he was no longer needed on this business, but could have back again his old job of foreman. Mace had been a fool and he was glad to be rid of him.

The thing was too big, too, to let a man like White stand in his way; $30,000 was involved here, and the job was three-quarters finished. This Hugh Conner was another stumbling block, but Keyes already knew how to take care of him. With old man White and Hugh Conner out of the way, he could end this in a hurry. The main thing was the need of ending the deal at once, before too many people became suspicious. There was the burning of Conner's layout as clear proof that someone already suspected what was going on. Had Conner touched off that blaze himself? No, the man was too stubborn to burn the roof over his head when he could stay and fight.

After he had eaten, Keyes spoke to his men: "You three were hired at a hundred a month, and I told you it was fightin' wages. Tonight I'll prove that. We're ridin' back to White's place."

He eyed them individually—Slim with his unreadable thin face and cold caramel-colored eyes; Tony whose long nose and full lips gave a hint of his Indian ancestry; and Blazer whose huge body dwarfed the other two and whose ugly pockmarked face and ham-like fists and brawny strength had made him a killer before turning fifteen. Keyes knew his men and now drawled: "Whatever happens tonight puts us all in the same buggy. I don't think I'll have to worry about any of you talkin'."

"Let's get on with it," Blazer growled, voicing the opinion of the others.

An hour later Keyes looked down on Ben White's place, shadowy in the starlit darkness. He waited impatiently, watching the cabin's single, lighted window, wondering how long it would take Blazer to make the first move.

It came sooner than he expected, a hoarse, piercing cry from out of the trees in front of the cabin. Keyes transferred his glance to the cobalt-shadowed porch, waiting for the one happening that was beyond his control. When the door opened to throw a shaft of orange light over the porch and the yard, he breathed a sigh of relief.

It was better than he had hoped for. Ben White came out of his door holding a lighted lantern high over his head, peering out into the night.

"Who's there?" White called out, and the words were hardly out of his mouth before Tony's shape darted into the circle of light behind him. White's choked, startled cry drifted out across the night and his knees suddenly buckled and he dropped the lantern, snuffing out its light so that only the duller glow of lamplight from inside brought out the details. Tony caught the rancher as he fell, and lifted and dragged him in through the door, out of sight.

Slim appeared out of the darkness and walked across the porch and into the cabin, shutting the door behind him. Inside, he helped Tony lift White, whose eyes were already glazing, to his bunk. They took off his boots and threw his blankets over him, and Slim even thought to take the rancher's pipe out of his pocket and put it on the chair alongside the bunk.

Tony brought the lamp over and set it on the chair. Then, giving it a gentle shove, he watched it topple to the floor with a *crash* as both base and chimney shattered. The wick guttered out, so Slim wiped a match alight on the seat of his trousers and flicked it into the spreading pool of coal oil. The flame caught in a pungent, black cloud of smoke, then spread and licked up along the blankets until they suddenly burst into flame.

"That'll do," Slim said, watching Tony wipe the blood off his knife on a corner of the blankets. "Walk on your toes on the way out and stick to the path. The boss said we weren't to leave tracks."

"Not my tracks," Tony breathed, and made his way across the wavily lighted room to the door.

They met the others on the trail below.

"Everything all right?" Keyes queried, as they swung in alongside his pony.

Slim grinned. "Slick as a whistle, boss."

VII

At twenty minutes past nine that same night Walt Andrews took out his watch and looked at it, and then across his office at his deputy. "It's time," he said. "You've got the horses saddled? You're sure he doesn't know you?"

Hugh nodded and got up out of his chair. "He doesn't. On the way back I thought I'd like to swing up into the valley to my place. I forgot and left the corral gate shut. Those bronc's ought to be on the loose until I get back up there for good."

"Go ahead. There won't be anything doing around here in the morning."

Hugh left the office, and for two full minutes Walt Andrews sat staring at the door, elbows on the arms of his chair, one hand slowly fingering his grizzled mustache. At length he reached down and opened a drawer beside him and took out a sheaf of Reward posters and fingered through them until he found the one he wanted. He put it on the desk before him and returned the others to the drawer. For the tenth time that day he read that poster.

He gave a long, subdued sigh and abruptly rose and crumpled the dodger and took it over to the stove, raising the lid and dropping it onto the hot coals inside. Then he came back to the desk and sat down and laboriously penciled a note which was addressed to a Montana sheriff and which read:

Have you further information to add to Reward notice dated March of this year regarding killer of Wade Henderson?

Finished, he reached to the peg on the wall behind his desk and took down his Stetson and put it on. He banked the fire in the stove, opened the check draft, and blew out the lamp and went outside. On his way to the station to send his telegram, he looked in through the hotel doors. Hugh Conner was talking to the oldster behind the desk.

Hugh was saying: "Is Riley in?"

The clerk nodded. "Room Twenty."

Hugh went on up the steps. He knocked at the door of room *20* and heard a chair scrape inside. Then Summers's voice queried: "Who is it?"

"Keyes sent me."

The door opened and Summers stood there with a gun in his hand hanging at his side. He jerked his head and Hugh stepped in, closing the door behind him.

"Were you expecting Mace Dow?" Hugh asked, grinning as he observed the wicked-looking short-barreled gun Summers carried.

Summers nodded: "How did you know?"

Instead of answering the question, Hugh voiced another guess: "That's why I came. About Mace, I mean. He's been proddy all day because he didn't get taken along. Keyes thought you ought to be moving out of here to a safer place."

"You mean that Mace . . . ?"

"I mean that it would be easy for Mace to crawl onto that roof outside and blow a hole through you if he wanted. He's ornery."

Summers's eyes became narrow-lidded, flared with suspicion. "Who are you? What do you know?"

"All there is to know. You're Summers of the Sierra Central and the boss is helping you swing the deal for buying up the valley that leads to that low pass up by Wind River. Isn't that enough?"

Summers laughed, not heartily, for he had been put under a terrible strain in the last minute. "What does Keyes want me to do?"

"Get your stuff packed, leave money on the table for your room, and come along with me. We'll go down the back way. I've got two ponies waiting out in the alley. We'll get out of town without anyone seeing you and let Mace do what he likes about it."

Summers worked quickly, packing his belongings in his one bag. He left a $5 gold piece on the bureau, blew out the lamp, and they went down the back stairs. When they had ridden along the alley to its end and were suddenly in open country, the town behind them, Summers queried: "Where are you taking me?"

"It's a long ride. You'll see."

After two hours of steady going along the trail that angled south and east from Bull Forks, Summers shifted uncomfortably in his saddle and asked impatiently: "How much farther?"

"Another hour."

They rode on in silence for a while, until Hugh said abruptly: "There's some of us who don't think we're getting enough out of this deal. Take Mace, for instance. Keyes has used him for fifteen years and now he throws him down like a worn-out pair of boots." The one thing Hugh had to go on was what George Baird had overheard Summers say that morning and the belief that Wyatt Keyes had gone a little too far in using Mace, and that doubtless he regretted it now. A man like Keyes wouldn't waste time trying to swing an understrapper into line, for it was a simple matter to find an efficient man to ramrod an outfit like the Key-Bar.

"Keyes never should have trusted Mace," Summers said.

Then, silent a moment, he queried: "Did Keyes give you any word to bring to me?"

"Only to get back to Denver as quick as you can and to wait to hear from him."

"Back to Denver?"

Hugh nodded, pointed ahead, to where a half dozen pinpoints of light winked out in the distance. "That's Colgate. I'm to see that you leave on the midnight train."

"But this. . . ." Summers stubbornly clamped his jaw shut after those two words. It was a full five minutes later that he said: "Keyes wouldn't be fool enough to try to reach me by wire. I've warned him about that. He'd lay the whole thing wide open if he did. All wires come direct to the office and a copy is put on open file. I'd be cashiered the minute it was delivered. I'm supposed to be down here doing this on my own."

Hugh looked across at the man, saw the beads of perspiration standing out on his forehead. He chuckled softly and said: "I wouldn't worry."

But Summers did worry. While they waited in the gloomy shed that served as the Colgate way station, he penciled a note that he gave Hugh to deliver to Keyes.

Forty minutes later they flagged the train, using the red lantern that hung inside the shed for that purpose. Summers climbed onto the last coach, pausing on the step long enough to tell Hugh: "There's something I forgot to mention. If that man White wouldn't sell today, tell Keyes to double the two-hundred-dollar limit. We'll split the loss between us."

The locomotive cut loose with two sharp blasts of its whistle and the coaches started moving. Hugh's last look at the man showed him a face robbed of its color to a pallid, worried tenseness.

When the lantern swinging from the end of the last coach had faded into the darkness, Hugh opened the note Summers had given him. He flicked alight a match and held it over the scrap of paper, reading:

In case you want to reach me, wire my sister, Miss Anne Summers, 27 County Road, Denver. This business must be finished by the end of next week, otherwise I advise Sierra Central to use their option on the lower pass before it expires.

G. Summers

With that last bit of information Hugh pieced together the last links of this chain of evidence damning Wyatt Keyes.

One remark of Summers stayed in his mind. *If that man White wouldn't sell today, tell Keyes to double the two hundred dollar limit.* That would be Ben White, up at the head of the valley. So Ben had been stubborn?

Knowing Keyes and his ways, Hugh felt a vague alarm over this news. If Ben White wouldn't sell, then Keyes would use other means. Why not ride up and have a talk with Ben and warn him? So thinking, Hugh tied the reins of Summers's horse to the saddle horn and led the animal a half mile down the Bull Forks road before he turned him loose. Then he cut north from the trail with an all-night ride ahead of him.

If Hugh thought he and Summers had left the hotel unseen, he was mistaken. Mace, who had been drinking all day at Faro Mike's after Keyes's curt order to report at the Key-Bar the following day, had been on his way across the street to the lunch room for a late supper when he saw Hugh entering the hotel. Sight of the man who was chiefly responsible for his falling from Keyes's good graces brought up a killing lust within Mace. He followed Hugh into the hotel and asked the clerk where he had gone.

When the oldster answered—"He's up in Room Twenty with Riley."—Mace had given away to his disbelief for one instant, and then realized fully what this meant. Here was a way to buy back into Keyes's favor once more.

He went into the upper hallway and hid in the shadow of the stairwell until Hugh and Summers left the room. He followed them down into the alley and out of town. He went back for his horse and made a wide circle to the Colgate trail and saw them ride past an hour later. Two hours after that, he hunkered down in a mesquite thicket less than twenty yards from the station and saw Hugh flag the midnight train. After the train pulled out, he watched while Hugh read the note by the light of a match. And twenty minutes after Hugh turned Summers's horse loose on the Bull Forks trail, Mace overtook the animal.

For a long ten seconds a cold fear took hold of him at the thought that Hugh might have seen him and be waiting along the trail ahead. But then he reasoned that, if Hugh had discovered his presence and was waiting, he wouldn't have let this pony go the way he had.

He rode past the riderless bronco, putting his own animal into a swinging run, muttering: "Goddlemighty, will Wyatt be glad to see me this time."

VIII

It was an hour after sunup when Hugh rounded the head of the trail to look on Ben White's place. A neat two-room cabin had stood proudly in the niche the thick cedars made against the abrupt slope of the hills up ahead. But now that cabin was gone, and in its place was a pile of charred, smoking timbers that was mute evidence of what had happened.

Hugh felt something within him harden and turn cold. It was a full half minute before he put down the nausea that gripped him and spurred up the trail to where a man stood looking at him from alongside the cabin's ruins.

He knew what he would find even before he asked the man,

Jeff Wilke, White's nearest neighbor: "What happened, Jeff?"

Wilke was a bear-like man, thick-framed, short, and with a bushy black beard that gave him a pugnacious look even though he was mild-mannered and soft-spoken. He lifted his sloping shoulders in a shrug. "I wouldn't know, Hugh. I spotted this blaze at eight or thereabouts last night. Me and the missus hitched up the team and drove here as fast as we could. It was blazin' like a stack o' dry hay. Hell, we couldn't've got in to him even if we had known."

"He was in there?"

Wilke nodded and turned to let his glance run over the burned, upended line of timber lengths that marked the remains of the partition dividing the cabin into its two rooms. "We've had a look, Hugh. It wasn't nice. As near as we can make out, old Ben went to sleep with the lamp burnin'. It tipped off his chair. He's in what's left of his bunk. There's a couple of legs left of the chair, near the bunk. His blankets were over him because he was layin' on part of 'em . . . the part that didn't burn. His pipe was there alongside the chair . . . the only damned thing that's supposed to burn and didn't. You can take a look if you want, but you won't eat for a week if you do."

Hugh swung down out of the saddle and had a look around the yard. "Anyone come up here yesterday or last night?"

"Keyes and three of his hardcases were up here to have a talk with Ben. I know, because they stopped at my place and Keyes paid me my money and told me he aimed to call on Ben."

"Then you sold out?"

"What the hell else could a man do? Keyes has ways of makin' us sell. I'm a family man, Hugh, and I don't aim to mix in with what I can see comin' for those who don't jump at the crack of his whip."

"Was Ben going to sell?"

"He wasn't. He told me so two, three days ago." Wilke

frowned as the gradual dawning of an idea took root in his mind. "Say! Do you figure Keyes came back and . . . ?"

"I don't figure a thing."

Wilke's look turned from worried perplexity to a grim soberness. "I sent Johnny Davis in after the sheriff. Maybe we ought to get a bunch together and ride over to the Key-Bar."

Hugh shook his head. "And what good would that do us without proof? No, what I want you to do is to keep everyone away from the place until Walt Andrews gets here. I'm riding down to my corral to turn some stock loose. I'll be back. You're in charge here while I'm gone. Have you got a gun?"

Wilke swept his sheepskin aside, exposing the cedar-handled butt of a six-gun he had thrust in the waistband of his trousers. "I've been carryin' this for a week now."

"There'll be others coming along to see what happened as soon as the news gets around. Keep 'em away until Andrews has a chance to look over the cabin and the yard. And you might be careful about spreading your tracks around, Jeff. I don't think we'll get much from sign, but there's always a chance."

Hugh mounted and rode on down the trail. He began to feel a slow weariness settling through him, and abruptly realized how little rest he had had in the past three days. Excitement had supplied him with the energy for last night's ride, but now he was dog-tired.

"Keyes did it," he muttered, half aloud. Yet as firmly as the conviction took hold of him, just as firmly did he know that there would be no evidence, no proof the law could get to warrant an arrest. The word of the Key-Bar riders would carry as much weight before law, probably more, than any amount of weak evidence the sheriff could supply. Keyes had covered his tracks well.

A half hour later he approached the spot where he had met

Fay Baird two days ago, the margin of trees that circled the upper end of his pasture. Remembrance of her was somehow refreshing. After all, his being in on this was a thing of her doing. The girl had fire, probably a measure of those same qualities of her father's that had gone to seed during the past few years. Just now he felt a grim hopelessness at realizing that someday soon he might have to be leaving this country—outriding the law as he had done once before. His luck couldn't hold.

He was leaving the trees and heading down into his pasture when a voice suddenly rang out close at hand: "Conner!"

He stiffened in his saddle and dropped his right hand to his side as he turned to search out that voice. Wyatt Keyes stood thirty feet away, his back to the trunk of a tall cedar, a rifle half raised to his shoulder.

"Look behind you before you make a try for it," Keyes warned tonelessly.

A strange and pervading sense of defeat had already gripped Hugh as he turned and looked to his other side. Mace Dow and the stolid, burly Blazer had ridden out of the trees, each holding a six-gun that was lined at him.

"Shuck out your irons, Conner! One at a time!"

Hugh was careful to time his motions to an agonizing slowness, knowing the men who faced him. When his guns were on the ground, Keyes said: "Slim, come on out and tie him on."

A fourth man appeared, a stranger to Hugh. The grin on his thin face was belied by the brittle quality in his peculiar, light-colored eyes. He stepped out with a rope in his hands, and stooped over and flicked the noosed end of it onto Hugh's right boot. And then Hugh rolled out of the saddle.

A gun *crashed* out behind him, searing a burn along his left shoulder. He reached down and his two hands closed on Slim's neck as his weight crashed down on the man. He chopped in a hard blow that caught him behind the ear, then groped down wildly to reach the man's holstered six-gun.

His fingers closed on the handle and he swung the gun clear and thumbed back the hammer and met Blazer's rush with a blasting shot that stopped the man and sent him sinking in a loose sprawl to the ground. Hugh looked around, saw Keyes, and was swinging the weapon into line when Mace Dow's chopping downstroke from behind wiped the barrel of a six-gun across his temples in a bone-crushing blow that sent him into unconsciousness.

IX

Fay Baird and her father were in Walt Andrews's office that morning when Johnny Davis rode in with the news of Ben White's death.

Andrews took it stoically, frowning as Johnny finished. "Any idea how it started, Johnny?"

"Only that busted lamp alongside his bunk."

"Anyone up there last night?"

"Only Jeff Wilke. He was too late."

"I mean was there anyone up there to see Ben before it happened?"

"Keyes and two or three of his men rode past my place early in the afternoon."

Andrews's eyes took on a granite-like quality. He got up out of his chair and reached for his hat and looked at George Baird and said: "You coming?"

"Of course he is," Fay Baird answered, rising to follow the sheriff.

"Wait a minute, Walt!" Baird called out. "Why should we go up there with you?"

Andrews's look was one of disgust. "You mean you can't guess the answer?"

With a flush of color rising in under his tan, George Baird

said quietly: "You'll have to prove it to me, Walt."

Out on the walk, as they were climbing into their saddles, a man called out from down the street: "Walt, here's a wire for you."

It was the station agent. He came up and handed a telegram to Walt Andrews, asking: "Any answer?"

The lawman tore open the message, let the hint of a satisfied smile break in on his sober expression as he read the message, then tucked it into his pocket, and said: "No answer, Wade."

They left town at a fast trot and rode that way for nearly two hours, until at noon they swung into sight of Hugh's place in the valley. When Andrews saw the three ponies in the corral, he frowned and told Fay, who was riding beside him: "That's funny. He said he'd be up here this morning."

He got down out of the saddle and swung open the corral gate and let the horses out to water. Looking up at the ruins of the cabin and wagon shed, he smiled thinly and remarked: "Hugh did a good job of it." Then he turned to Davis. "Johnny, if you can spare the time, I'd like you to wait here for Hugh. Bring him on up to White's if he gets here in the next hour or two."

Davis nodded: "I ain't got a thing to do, Walt. Go ahead."

At White's they met Jeff Wilke. He gave them the story he had given Hugh earlier that morning, and ended by saying: "Hugh ought to be back any minute. He rode on down to his place to turn his stock out to water."

Walt Andrews, who had been gazing soberly at the ruins of the cabin, whirled to face him. "Hugh's been here this morning?"

Wilke nodded, his glance puzzled.

"But we came that way looking for him," Fay Baird protested. She had lost a little color during the last few minutes as she listened to Wilke's story and looked out upon the burned cabin.

But now his words brought a flush coursing up over her regular features: "That means, Dad, . . . it means something's happened to him. Don't you see, if he started down there. . . ."

"Wilke, go back to your place and saddle a horse and ride down the valley and get every man you can," Walt Andrews said in sudden decision. "Get Johnny Davis. We left him at Hugh's place. We're ridin' for the Key-Bar. You'll meet us there in two hours if you have to kill your jugheads doin' it." He turned to George Baird. "I'm not askin' you two to ride there with me. There may be trouble, then again I may be making a wrong guess. But if anything's happened to Hugh, it's an even bet Keyes is mixed up in it."

It wasn't Baird who answered, but his daughter. "I'm coming, Walt. And I think Dad will, too." She cast a sidelong glance at her father, wondering what his answer would be.

George's leathery countenance had undergone a change during the past few moments. There was a hard light in his eyes that his daughter had never before seen, but that Walt Andrews remembered from years ago. The lawman smiled grimly, said: "I'd have walked up here on my hands to see you come around, George."

Baird reached around and undid the flap of his saddlebag and took out a long-barreled Colt .38 and rammed it into his belt. When they rode back down the trail, he was leading the way at a stiff run.

X

The Key-Bar bunkhouse was long and low, a native adobe house converted to Keyes's use. A crude pine table and four benches took up the room's center, while a double tier of bunks, sixteen in all, filled the entire length of the back wall. They threw Hugh Conner into one of these, his hands and feet laced together. Mace and Keyes and Slim brought him in.

Outside, a man's steps sounded, running across the yard. A moment later he appeared in the bunkhouse door. "Someone comin' in along the trail, boss."

Keyes said: "You guard the door, Slim. Don't let anyone in. Mace, better come with me."

Keyes rounded the corner of his big stone house and stopped, scanning the faint ribbon of the Bull Forks trail. A half mile away were three riders. "Looks like Andrews and Baird and his girl. Mace, they may know more than we think. You round up the crew and tell 'em to spread through the house and around the bunkhouse. If Andrews tries to make a play, they're to stop him."

Ten minutes later Keyes was standing on the steps of the porch, his smile affable, looking out at his three visitors. "Get down and come in," he invited. Baird's look was fixed severely on Keyes, and Andrews was lacking his usual smile; even the girl's glance was vaguely accusing, so Keyes queried: "Anything wrong?"

"Keyes, I want to take a look through your house," Andrews said. "Hugh Conner disappeared this morning on the way between Ben White's place and his own. You reckon you could explain that?"

"You mean do I know where he went, Walt? No."

"I'll have a look, anyway." Andrews swung down out of his saddle. "Come on, George."

"Just a minute!" Keyes said. "You can't go in there, Walt. Not without a search warrant. If you'd come here as friends and wanted a look through the layout, you'd be welcome. But when you hang a thing like this on me without reason, when you decide to blame me for every forked play that's made in this country, you aren't welcome. First you blamed this fire of Conner's onto me. I didn't do it. Now it's this other. You ride back to town and get yourself a search warrant and I'll listen."

"You wouldn't know about Ben White being killed and his place burned last night, would you, Keyes?"

There wasn't a trace of emotion to betray Keyes. "White's place fired?" He even managed a scornful laugh. "Next you'll be sayin' I did that."

"Keyes, I'm going to look this place over whether you like it or not. Come on, George." The sheriff suddenly walked toward the porch. George Baird followed, and Keyes stepped aside to let them pass, a smug smile heightening his arrogance.

Andrews turned the knob on the door and threw it open, then stopped. Four feet inside the house's big living room stood a Key-Bar rider with a double-barreled shotgun slung from the crook of his arm. Andrews took one step inside and the rider silently raised the muzzle of his weapon. Andrews stopped once more and turned to face Keyes. "So that's the way it is?"

Keyes shrugged. "I said you weren't welcome, Walt. Ride back for a search warrant."

Baird, more impulsive than his friend, pushed past Walt and into the room. The man with the gun put one hand around the stock, the other on the barrel grip of the gun, lined it at Baird, and breathed: "Don't make me let this thing off, friend."

"Hold on, George," Andrews growled as he saw Baird's hand start edging toward his six-gun. "There's plenty of time for this. We can always come back."

He took Baird by the arm and led him back to their ground-haltered ponies, and both men went into the saddle, and Andrews led the way out of the yard, ignoring Keyes as best he could.

When they were through the pasture gate, Keyes went inside his office. Mace was waiting there. "Let 'em get out of sight over the hill, Mace. Then you take a *pasear* back along the trail and make sure they didn't leave anyone to watch the layout. As soon as you're back, you're headed for the north line shack.

You'll take Conner up there and I can let Andrews have his look at this place this afternoon when he gets back from town."

Two minutes later Mace rode out of the yard. Keyes watched him make a mile-wide circle, inwardly satisfied at the way his ramrod was going about his job. It looked like Mace was coming around; the ex-sheriff had done a nice piece of work last night in following Hugh and Summers to Colgate, and Keyes was thinking that Summers had been wrong, that he wasn't through with Mace after all. It wasn't every day a man could find an understrapper like Mace—one who would shut his eyes to the right thing and wasn't squeamish about doing a few dirty jobs.

But half an hour later, still standing there on the porch, it took two seconds for Keyes to change his mind about Mace. He saw his ramrod top the far rise along the trail and ride in toward the house, leading another horse. That horse was Fay Baird's chestnut, and even at this distance Keyes could see the girl lying across the withers of Mace's horse, ahead of his saddle. By the time Mace swung into the yard, Keyes was nursing a temper that had taken the color from his face and was making his black eyes narrow-lidded and beady.

Mace smiled crookedly and called out: "Look what I found hunkered down behind a tree up the trail, boss! She wouldn't come along peaceable, so I tied her up." He swung down and lifted the girl to the ground, steadying her with one hand to keep her from falling. Fay Baird's hands and feet were tied, her hair was mussed, and her clothes were smeared with dust. "She put up a good scrap," Mace said, laughing softly.

Then he saw the look on Keyes's face, and sobered instantly. Keyes came down off the porch and stood in front of his ramrod. "How much have you told her?"

"All there is to know," Fay Baird said, her chin tilted defiantly. "I know you have Hugh Conner here and that you fired Ben

White's place. You'll all hang, Wyatt Keyes!"

Keyes's hand flashed out in an open-handed blow that caught Mace fully in the mouth. "So you told her," he purred. His right hand closed on the butt of his gun. "I ought to fill your gutless belly with slugs, you sidewinder."

Mace swallowed hard, fear riding into his glance. "Hold on, boss. I swear I didn't tell her a thing. I just found her up there watchin' the layout and brought her back like you said. She made all this up."

"But if you had half a brain. . . ."

Keyes broke off abruptly, his rage holding him speechless. At length, he cooled down enough to say: "This is the worst play you could have made. Now they'll know for sure." He stood a moment, trying to think above the rising urge that made him want to kill Mace Dow. He would take care of Mace later, he reasoned, for with Fay Baird on his hands, not daring to let her go because of what she knew, he might have need of every gun he could get before long. Or maybe he could make a deal with Walt Andrews—a deal that would be an exchange of his life for the girl's. But he'd have to leave the country unless he played his cards right.

A shout from out by the bunkhouse cut in on his thoughts. He looked over there to see a man pointing up the trail. Keyes's glance whipped around to see, far out, a knot of horsemen swinging toward the layout in a boil of dust.

"Get her into the bunkhouse along with Conner!" Keyes rasped. "You have one more chance, Mace. Step out o' line and I'll know what to do! Tell Slim and the others to meet me in the office. You stay at the bunkhouse."

Mace picked up the girl and ran awkwardly toward the bunkhouse, while Keyes went into his office.

Two minutes later, looking through a pair of binoculars, he had identified Jeff Wilke and Johnny Davis in the group of eight riders. Shortly they all stopped well out of range, and Wilke called across: "We saw the girl, Keyes! Turn her loose, or we'll surround the place and smoke you out!"

Keyes didn't bother to shout back an answer. Reason told him that Wilke and his men would be careful, knowing that something might happen to the girl if they carried out their threat. But the chance was gone now of leaving for the line camp. They were cornered.

But there's the girl and there's the deputy, he mused, walking back into his office. *And Walt Andrews never broke his word to a man. This isn't over yet.*

XI

Hugh had been lying there for ten minutes now, his head aching until the pain of it drove him half mad. He had heard voices out there a few minutes ago—Walt Andrews's and Wyatt Keyes's voices—and he had questioned Slim, who stood guard at the door. Slim would talk, and did, seeming to take a grim satisfaction in turning Hugh's hopelessness to a bottomless despair. So when Mace brought Fay to the bunkhouse and threw her roughly into the bunk alongside, Hugh knew more than a little of what had gone on.

Mace told Slim: "The boss wants you up at the office. I'll watch these two."

After Slim had left, Hugh heard the girl say: "This about finishes you with Wyatt Keyes, Dow."

Mace whirled to face her, his pent-up anger giving away before a string of oaths. "That'll be enough out of you, sister!"

A moment later Hugh said: "Mace, the two of us could swing this together."

"Swing what?"

The worry that showed on Mace's gaunt face gave Hugh his cue.

"Keyes is through with you, like she says. Why don't you make your own play and leave the country before you get a bullet in the back?"

"Who said Keyes was through with me?"

Fay Baird laughed mockingly—a laugh that brought Mace whirling around in a hot fury to face the sound of her voice.

Hugh spoke before Mace could give vent to the violence that was building up inside him. "I had it straight from Summers that he and Keyes were ready to get rid of you. Is that proof enough?"

"That was yesterday. Today Keyes thinks different."

"Not after you brought me in," Fay said. Somehow, she had caught the drift of Hugh's remarks.

"Mace, I tallied you as being wise. A wise man wearing your boots would clear out. But when you do clear out, I say you and I ought to cash in on this thing."

"You and me? How?"

"What would George Baird pay to get his girl back?"

"Hugh!" Fay was incredulous.

"Don't listen to her," Hugh told Mace. "Get what I have to say. Keyes will hold the girl until Walt Andrews and George Baird come to his terms. Keyes may even collect a little money on her . . . to make up for what he's going to have to lose now that he can't buy up the valley for the railroad. He'll leave the country. But it's a three-to-one bet that he won't take care of you, Mace. He may even turn you over to the law."

"You're loco," Mace scoffed. "I know too much about Keyes. I'll talk."

"Then he'll measure you for a pine nightshirt and not take any chances. You're through, Mace." Hugh paused a second, letting his words sink in. "What we ought to do is get out of here tonight . . . with your help it'll be easy . . . and take the girl and strike north into the hills and make our own deal with

Baird and Andrews. With twenty thousand to split between us, we could leave the country and still be ahead of the game."

A shrewd look had crept into Mace's glance. "Supposin'," he said, "just supposin' I'd sell out on Keyes. What makes you think I'd swing you in on it, friend?"

"You'd have to. Neither Baird nor Andrews would deal with you. They don't trust you, Mace. By the time you convinced them you had the girl, Keyes's crew would have hunted you down. But with me in on it, we can finish the whole thing in a day or so . . . while Keyes is still cooped up here. Both the tin star and old man Baird trust me. They'll do what I say. It's worth twenty thousand, Mace. Think it over."

"You go to hell," was Mace's cautious answer, his words belied by the greedy light that came to his eyes. "I always did wonder about you, Conner. You're plenty shifty."

"When I have to be."

They heard steps approaching across the yard, and a moment later Slim appeared in the doorway. "The boss says for me to stay with these two, Mace." Slim's tone was no longer respectful. Keyes had told him a few things.

Mace left without a word, and Hugh lay there for minutes wondering if he had carried his point. Once he rolled onto his side, so that he could look across at Fay. She managed a smile and whispered: "You didn't really mean it, did you, Hugh?"

He laughed softly. "Part of it."

"Which part?"

"Wait and see."

XII

Walt Andrews and George Baird came back from town shortly before dark. Slim, standing in the doorway, told Hugh and Fay how the sheriff stopped on the crest of the rise up the trail to talk to Jeff Wilke and his men. Later, Andrews came halfway to the house and called to Keyes, and the Key-Bar owner, surrounded by four of his men, walked out and had a long talk with the lawman. Andrews didn't come back to the house with him.

After supper, when Slim came back on duty, he gave Hugh the news. "Andrews didn't like the boss' proposition. So he's out there, with his posse covering the layout, trying to think of a way to get you two loose." Slim chuckled. "Maybe he'll feel different in the morning."

The night wore on, slowly for Hugh, for each moment he expected to be hearing from Mace. This was their only chance, and, unless Mace did his part, they might never get out of here alive. Slim, good-natured and obliging, several times rolled cigarettes for Hugh. He wasn't worrying and Hugh knew that the man reflected Keyes's confidence.

Shortly after 10:00 it happened. Mace came to the door and told Slim: "Time for coffee. The boss says for me to stick around while you're up at the cook shanty. Be back in ten minutes."

Slim hesitated, suspicion flaring in his glance. But finally his eyes lost their hardness, and he gave a thin smile and leaned his rifle against the door frame and sauntered out into the darkness. They listened to the sound of his steps receding across the yard, then Mace said quickly: "Keyes has got his guards all around the layout. Barn, sheds, corral." He stepped over to Hugh and bent down quickly and slashed at his ropes with a knife. Then he crossed over to Fay and had her on her feet in a quarter of a minute. He took out one of his guns and handed it to Hugh. "We'll cut out back for the wagon shed. There's no time to saddle ponies, so we'll head across that field out back and make for the trees on that far hill."

He turned down the lamp, went to the door and looked out, then signaled them to follow, and disappeared into the darkness outside. Hugh was stiff and sore from lying in one position for so long, and it was several seconds before he could reach out to steady Fay and walk awkwardly to the door with his hand holding her arm. As he went out with her, he reached down and got Slim's rifle. Outside, they made out the shadow of Mace's figure in the darkness ahead. Hugh walked quickly now, coming closer to the Key-Bar ramrod. Ahead, the bulk of the wagon shed loomed blackly in the shadows.

Hugh jerked open the door and pushed Fay inside as someone at the far corner of the building called out a strident challenge. Hugh made out the guard's figure and lifted the Colt Mace had given him and thumbed one shot that blasted across the silence. The man's shadowy outline sank to the ground, and Hugh lunged through the door into the building just as other shots crashed out from up at the house. He took one last glimpse out across the yard and saw Mace's lean frame sprawled loosely on the ground twenty feet away. Mace wasn't moving out of that ungainly sprawl; he was dead.

Shouts shuttled out across the still air, and from down by the barn someone with a rifle set up a careful, even firing that whipped lead through the wagon shed's door. As that first bullet splintered the wood sheathing, Hugh flicked alight a match and looked quickly around.

Fay stood ten feet ahead of him, in the center of the shed's open dirt floor. There was a litter of gear strewn along the right-hand side, broken bridles, harness, and a buggy's gaunt chassis backed into a far corner. Along the left-hand wall was stacked a waist-high pile of twelve-inch planks. Hugh's match flickered out and he lit another and told Fay: "Get down behind that lumber."

He held the light long enough for her to make a place for herself between the lumber and the side wall, then, with a quick look around, he threw the match to the floor as other bullets found the mark of that door.

In his hasty glimpse toward the front he had seen a loose board near the base of the weathered frame wall, far to one side. He felt his way toward it now, once feeling the air whip of a bullet as it tore through the siding and rushed past his face. Finally he found the board and tore it loose and bellied down behind the small opening to look outside.

What he saw made him reach frantically for the rifle at his side. He had barely time to thrust its muzzle through the opening, to take aim, and to fire at the figure darting in out of the darkness at the wagon shed door. The running man out there broke his long stride and fell forward with a momentum that rolled him over twice before he lay still. Hugh had aimed at his chest.

Guns from up at the house set up an inferno of thunder, the low-pitched *crashes* of six-guns blending discordantly with the sharper explosions of the rifles. They hadn't spotted the opening at the base of the wall yet, but were covering the door with their shots.

Then, from farther away, he heard other guns; he listened for a full half minute, trying to identify those far sounds. Suddenly, from the darkness beyond the house's long, low shadow, he saw a distant wink of flame, then another beside it, and he turned and called back to Fay: "Andrews and your father are in it now!"

"Hugh, you must be careful." It was as though he hadn't mentioned the others.

Her tone, the low, intimate throb of her voice, set up in him a feeling that he had never before experienced. In that moment he knew that Fay Baird meant something more than a friend; her words, her thought had been for him alone. And in those few seconds, he knew that he had found the one thing in life that mattered to him. He had found it and would lose it, for if he came through this night alive, he would have to face the same thing he had been facing for days now, for months—the knowledge that the dark trails held his future, that he could never again live his life the way he would have chosen.

Abruptly the shots from the house died out. In a few moments the rifles of the posse that had been throwing a steady fire at the house stopped firing, lacking the target of the gun flashes.

Through the settling silence, Keyes's voice sounded from the near side of the house. "Take a look, Red. I think we got 'em."

Hugh's glance shuttled to the barn, fifty feet away and to one side. He saw a moving shadow at the barn door, saw a man come out of it, and carefully walk the length of the wall until he suddenly cut out and ran directly across toward the wagon shed. From in back of the barn, at the far limits of the pasture, a gun cut loose in two quick bursts that sent puffs of dust striking up at the running man's heels.

Then he was in the shelter of the wagon shed and that far gun broke off its firing and the silence was heavy-laden.

Hugh watched the shadow of Red's legs cross before the opening where he lay. Then the man was fumbling with the hasp at the door, pulling it open.

Red took two steps inside, stood listening against the ominous silence. Then Hugh said softly: "I've got a gun on you, Red!"

The lighter shade of the ground through the open doorway outlined Red's suddenly stiffening frame. He whirled around, blurring up a gun in a sudden, beating explosion of sound. Hugh pressed the trigger of his rifle, sure of his aim, and Red's stocky form jerked, he gave a low moan, and slowly toppled forward on his face. Hugh was on him a second later, wrenching the guns from his already lifeless hands.

Hugh threw himself face down in the dirt as the rifles at the house blazed alive once more, drowning out the echoes of the suddenly renewed firing from the posse's guns. He crawled back to the opening and lay there, looking out once more.

Then, unexpectedly, some marksman in the barn began systematically throwing his shots at the base of the shed's front wall, working outward from the door. Hugh heard the bullets splitting the rough board siding and came to his knees with a momentary panic coursing through him. Suddenly a bullet whipped into him, low on his left side, and he half spun about before he lost his footing and lay there, breathing heavily on the floor. For one tense minute he waited, half paralyzed, expecting a second bullet to reach him each instant.

When it didn't come, he crawled back to the opening and scanned the yard once again. He was barely in time, for a man's outline showed almost directly before him running for the door of the shed. Hugh nosed out the rifle at an angle and fired one shot and the man's leaping run became an ungainly, forward sprawl.

They saw the powder flame of his gun, and now, an instant after he moved away, a dozen bullets searched out the opening and shredded the wood in the boards alongside. Hugh darted across the doorway to the other side of the building and pushed loose another board there, shoulder high, so that it gave him a six-inch-wide opening to look through. And time and again he thanked those marksmen on the hill who seemed to have sensed what was going on down here and were keeping Keyes's men bottled in the house and barn.

"Hugh! Hugh, are you there?" Fay called, a half hysteria edging her voice.

"Still here."

The next moment he was listening to the sound of running horses coming in from the south from the direction of the Bull Forks trail. That would be Walt Andrews and George Baird and the rest, and a wild surge of hope leaped alive in him.

Then, above the beat of those faraway pounding hoofs, Hugh

suddenly heard the *crunching* of boot soles on the gravel outside. A split second later, as he turned to face the door, a man's shadowy bulk loomed in the opening.

Some instinct guided that man's first blasting shot. As it momentarily lighted the shed's interior, Hugh saw another figure behind the first, saw the twisted, expectant expression on the face of the man who had fired. Hugh felt that first bullet gouge a searing burn low on his thigh, and then his own guns were beating out a double concussion that drove the man backwards through the opening in a falling lunge. The man behind dodged his companion's hurtling bulk and lunged in through the opening and to one side of the door.

Moving out of his first position, Hugh didn't dare trust himself to a shot, knowing that he might miss and expose his own hiding place. The gun thunder outside, now beating to a higher pitch, drowned out all the small noises that might have given him a cue to where the man stood. Cries and shouts up at the house told of the posse's arrival.

"I came down after you, Conner," a voice spoke out from across the shed. And even though the tone of that voice was muted by the explosions outside, Hugh recognized it as Keyes's. A stubborn pride and the knowledge that he had failed had brought Wyatt Keyes down here to hunt down the man who had ruined him. He could have ridden away without this last gesture, but he was choosing this way instead. And, grudgingly, Hugh felt a small admiration for the man.

"Where are you, Conner?" Keyes called out in an interval when the guns outside were momentarily stilled.

And when Hugh didn't answer, Fay Baird choked back a sob that was barely audible in the stillness.

"So the girl's alive, too," Keyes drawled, his voice already coming from another position.

Hugh's eyes were searching the darkness at the front wall, in the direction out of which Keyes's voice had sounded. His glance settled on the opening where he had torn loose the rotten board a few minutes ago. Through that long, rectangular opening showed a faint smear that was a patch of the lighter ground outside. Suddenly he saw a shadow blot out that faint blur of light, and in that split second he was arcing his guns into line.

He thumbed two shots at a point three feet above the opening, and, even as the light of the second blasting shot died out, he saw that he had failed, had given away his own position. For that burst of powder flare had showed him Keyes standing to the other side of the opening, his square face set in a shrewd smile. He had purposely thrust his foot out over it, standing well to one side.

Hugh lunged out of position once more, but, as he moved, Keyes's two guns blasted out an inferno of sound. Hugh went down under a crushing blow high up at his right shoulder, and from his knees he instinctively aimed at those gun flashes and worked the hammers of his .45s.

A faintness hit him so that it was hard to swing the weapons down as they bucked in his hands. Time and time again he blasted shots at those orange winks of gun flame, until at last his hammers *clicked* metallically on empty chambers.

He tried to get to his feet, but lacked the strength. So he sat there, knowing that he made a perfect target, waiting for the bullets to whip into him.

Outside men were shouting and horses crossed the hard-packed yard at a wild run. The sharp explosions of the rifles gave away to the deeper throb of six-guns. A door swung shut at the barn and a few moments later the yard was lit by the orange glow of flames. Someone had fired the barn.

Suddenly a figure was outlined in the doorway, and, as Hugh tried vainly to lift an empty Colt to cover the newcomer, a match flared alight, and Walt Andrews was standing there, looking down at him. The sheriff stepped back into the doorway and shouted: "Here they are, George! Bring a lantern."

A minute later, when George Baird, a smoking gun in one fist and a lantern in the other, stood looking at Fay and Hugh, Andrews called across from the far side of the shed: "Here's where I sign my first death certificate, George!"

Baird looked across and saw Wyatt Keyes's burly form lying awkwardly across a broken, upended keg. But what interested him most was that his daughter was in Hugh Conner's arms, her head against his chest.

Andrews saw it, too, and ran over to stand behind his friend.

Abruptly the lawman said: "Fay, Doc Painter's up at the house. I reckon it's safe for you to run up and get him. Hugh will need some fixing."

When she had gone out the door, Andrews reached into his pocket and took out the telegram he had received that morning and handed it to Hugh.

What it said was:

Don't bother to arrest Hugh Conner. Witnesses claim self-defense. Sorry no reward.

★ ★ ★ ★ ★

THE BULLET

★ ★ ★ ★ ★

Jon Glidden's original title for this story was "The Bullet." It was purchased by Popular Publications on April 1, 1948 and the author was paid $194. It appeared in *Fifteen Western Tales* (9/48) under the title "Dead Man's Sixes." For its appearance here in book form its title has been restored.

I

Tom Marolt reined on over toward the friendly glow of the livery barn's lantern, the slow *splashing* of his tired gelding's hoofs laying a harsh note over the sibilant metal whisper of the Mercantile's drain pipe disgorging the run-off. He rode head down and with wide shoulders hunched to put the poncho collar high at his neck against the slant of the drizzle, and water dripped steadily from the trough of his wide hat. He was chilled, weary to the bone, glad the long wet day was over.

The *bang* of his animal's shoes against the livery's plank ramp brought the kid hostler from the stove in the harness room and the youngster, seeing who it was, asked eagerly: "Any luck, Sheriff?"

"Not much, Bob."

The boy's expression changed quickly to one of undisguised disappointment. "The others drew a blank, too," he said in a small voice.

"So it goes." Tom Marolt eased his long frame stiffly down out of the saddle. "Better dry him off and give him some grain."

"Sure will." The boy spoke dejectedly and took the reins to lead the chestnut on back toward the gloom of the stalls.

Tom Marolt stood there idly rolling up his first dry smoke of the day, the chill depression in him warmed slightly by the youngster's concern. When he'd used the match, he found that the tobacco left a rank taste in his mouth, and, shortly throwing the weed away, he buckled the poncho tightly to his neck and headed out into the rain again, turning upstreet toward the lights of Clee Towers's eat shack.

He was halfway there when his stride broke, then continued on at sight of a man's high and wide shape turning out of a door farther on. As the other approached him, he tilted his head down, hoping he would pass unrecognized, not at all wanting to be stopped.

But the odds went against him as the other drew abreast, halted, and suddenly said: "That you, Tom?".

" 'Evening, Phil."

Knowing he couldn't ignore Phil Kirby, Tom stopped.

Kirby's full, handsome face showed a deep gravity in the faint light. "No luck, I suppose."

"Afraid not."

The other's sigh was plainly audible and his tone was harsh as he burst out: "Darn, why won't they let a man alone? Pay no attention to that editorial. Ed Tolliver's a sick man, ready to spill his bile at anyone. If it's worth anything for me to say it, Tom, you can count on me to go the limit for you."

"That's good to know," Tom drawled, only partially understanding. He was suddenly impatient to be by himself and lifted a hand, turning away, saying: "See you around."

"So long."

As he went on, he was keenly aware of the solid *clump* of Phil Kirby's boots fading behind him. Then shortly, abreast the restaurant, what Kirby had said made him change his mind about eating right away and sent him angling over the street, ignoring the cold feel of his boots and the way the mud sucked at them. Another light was drawing him now, this one shining feebly from a big window bearing the legend: *Custer County Clarion*.

Presently, kicking the mud from his boots at the far walk's edge, he was glancing in the print shop's windows, seeing a pale-haired girl sitting at a desk behind the low front counter. And the fact of her being there almost made him turn back.

What finally took him on in was stubbornly remembering that not so many months ago the sight of Sandy Tolliver would have drawn him rather than affect him as it did now. So he did his best to make his smile genuine as he closed the door and met her startled glance, drawling: "You're at it late, Sandy."

There was gladness in the look that replaced the girl's surprise. She nodded down to the littered desk. "Bills, Tom. Tomorrow's the First." She came up out of her chair, regarding him with a disconcerting warmth as she stepped to the counter opposite him. "We didn't expect you back while the storm lasted."

"No point in staying out in it." He reached inside the poncho and tossed a nickel to the counter. "Got an extra paper?"

She took a paper from a stack on her desk and opened it out, laying it before him and asking: "You . . . didn't find anything?"

Her hesitation brought a faint smile to his angular, deeply tanned features. "No one expected me to, did they?"

It gave him a contrary satisfaction to see the quick flush that came to her face. She made no direct reply, instead pointing to the right-hand column of the front page, telling him: "You're not going to like this."

He glanced at the column heading—*Where Is Our Law?*—more aware of her than of what he was reading. This tall girl with the straw-colored hair unsettled him to the point where his thinking was inclined not to come at all straight when he was around her. And the time was long gone when he could afford to give away to that feeling or let her know, even remotely, that she in any way stirred him.

So now he turned away to step over to the door and shrug out of his poncho, hanging it from a wall hook. He was faintly angry at his inability to put down this quickening interest in the girl, and, as he came back to the counter, he was careful not to look at her again. By the time his glance went to the paper once more, he was steadier, able to see the print and make sense of it.

After watching him for several moments she said gently: "Tom, I'm sorry about this. But Uncle Ed warned you it was coming."

"So he did."

The anger that was building in him now was of a different brand than that of a moment ago. The essence of the editorial was contained in the last paragraphs:

We have offered you these several instances where our cattle and horses have taken on 'wandering' and 'drifting' habits peculiar to range stock. As we go to press, word reaches us that our sheriff—elected by such a landslide last year—is out investigating still another complaint, this time having deputized a small posse to assist him.

If as before Tom Marolt returns empty-handed and with no explanation for the disappearance of this last bunch of cattle, we suggest that he appear before the meeting of the County Commissioners come next Thursday and try to convince them that he is earning his ninety a month.

The writer contends that our representative of the law is obligated to stop this rustling. What is he going to do about it?

Your Friend, The Editor

Thinking it through quite deliberately as he folded the paper and laid it aside, Tom realized that his relief was keener than his anger. Now it was out in the open—this enigma that had so completely baffled him these past months. He didn't like the way old Ed Tolliver had so publicly flaunted his shortcomings, yet, now that the issue had reached a showdown, it was better than the long uncertainty.

His taut-muscled expression made Sandy say in a hushed voice: "Of course he didn't mean it, Tom. He isn't himself. The doctor's terribly worried about his heart. If he has another bad attack, he may never live through it."

Tom's glance rose slowly to meet hers and the flinty look in his gray eyes made her add quickly: "He's cross with everybody. Today he even told Phil not to keep coming here so much to see me." The mention of Phil Kirby unsteadied her straightforward way of regarding him and she ended lamely: "So . . . try and understand, Tom."

"Where'll I find him?" he asked tonelessly.

"Don't see him tonight." A wide-eyed alarm touched her strong yet delicately molded features. "He's upset. Men have been coming in all day about this. One or two made him lose his temper."

"So I do have one or two friends?"

"Don't say that, Tom. Everyone understands."

Now, once again, he smiled, but his wintry expression hadn't eased as he drawled: "Met Phil on the street just now. He wanted me to know he was with me."

"Of course he is."

He noticed the confusion his words brought to her before he looked toward the unpainted partition closing off this front office. "Is Ed still in the shop?"

Instead of answering that she gave him a glance that was probing, yet no longer so thought revealing. "You don't like Phil, do you, Tom?"

The question was so unexpected that it jarred him, made him answer evasively: "Never thought of it one way or the other, Sandy."

"Oh, you've thought of it. I. . . ." She paused, still eyeing him in that straightforward, speculative way. Then: "You see, Tom, it matters what you think of him. It matters a great deal."

"Why should it?"

"He's asked me to marry him."

Unsurprised, he tried his best to crowd back that stirring of an emotion so long kept buried deeply inside him, yet now it came suddenly alive, making him want to ask her about the things that had been plaguing him these long months. How responsible was she for Phil Kirby's constant attentions? Did she ever think back on the old days before Phil had come here? Did she remember the dances at Harkness's mill, or last New Year's Eve when they drove through the snow to Lodgepole to have a breakfast at the hotel?

He wondered later just how he would have asked his questions. He was on the verge of it, that much he knew, when the hasp on the shop door *rattled* and the panel swung open on Ed Tolliver.

"Sandy, we got the type set up on those pamphlets for Kramer. What say we . . . ?"

Staring over his bifocals, the printer got that far before he saw Tom standing there beyond his niece. He jerked his head up, frowned, seemed about to go back through the door again. But he was a headstrong and stubborn man who didn't believe in retreat. So he closed the door with a *bang* and, eyeing Tom narrowly, asked: "How'd you like it?"

"The editorial?" Tom gave a slow smile. "A lot of truth to it. Ought to take the slack out of me, Ed."

The surprise that showed on Ed Tolliver's hawkish face was fleeting and he came on across to the counter, asking: "Who'd you bring in?"

"No one."

"Run onto anything at all?"

Tom took several seconds giving his answer. "Nothing I can mention just yet."

The muscles along the oldster's jaw stood out abruptly.

"Meaning I've got a loose tongue?"

"I didn't say that."

"The hell you. . . ."

"Ed," Sandy cut in quickly, "Tom's only saying that it's his own affair."

"The affairs of a sheriff are public property," Ed stated acidly. "Except for his strictly private business." He was glowering at Tom now, the telltale flush of an uncontrollable temper darkening his face as he added: "Damn a man that hides behind made-up words!"

"You can't say that to Tom," Sandy protested. "You can't. . . ."

"Easy, Sandy," Tom drawled. His glance went to the printer. "All right, Ed. You can have it for what it's worth. Remember last spring when that batch of cows and their calves went over the mountain from Dry Creek? When they found that stranger lying below that rim trail?"

"Sure I remember. Who doesn't?"

Tom absent-mindedly reached to the pocket of his jumper for tobacco. As he took it out and shook some from the sack onto a wheat-straw paper, he said: "Something I've never told anyone is that I had Len Price take pictures of the stranger's body, his face. They weren't too good but I sent them around anyway."

"Sent 'em where?"

"Down into New Mexico Territory,"

"Why there, for the love of God?"

"Just a hunch."

Ed Tolliver shook his head, lifting an ink-blackened hand to run through his thinning gray hair. "A man needs something to back a hunch."

"I had something to back mine."

"What?"

Tom seemed uncertain of himself now and glanced quickly at Sandy as he said: "Neither of you are going to like this."

"Suppose we don't?" came Ed's salty query. "I'm after facts. Be damned to hurt feelings."

"But I didn't have much to go on, Ed. Here's what it was. A week or so before what happened up Dry Creek I'd seen Bill Matthews in the hills sharing a camp with this stranger. Maybe you know I've not taken much to Bill. So I rode around their camp and went on."

Sandy's expression had gone impassive as he spoke and now Ed Tolliver, glancing at his niece, gave Tom a narrow, speculative glance and said: "Get this straight, Tom. If you've hooked Matthews in on anything underhanded, Phil Kirby's not to be dragged into it. Can a man help it if he hires a sidewinder?"

Tom lifted a hand with a spare gesture. "You're 'way ahead of me, Ed. Kirby probably doesn't know that's going on."

"And what is going on?"

Lifting his wide shoulders, Tom let out a slow sigh. "You tell me. I'd once heard Matthews remark that he'd been down in Las Cruces, so I pretty well covered that territory when I mailed these pictures of the stranger. I got some answers but only one that counted. It was from a U.S. Marshal. He'd known the stranger. Seems his name was Stringfellow. But what was more important was that he mentioned a man that sided Stringfellow down there, a wanted man. He described him."

When Tom hesitated, the printer asked: "Matthews?"

"It could have been."

For several moments Ed Tolliver stood staring at him bleakly, finally saying: "Go ahead."

"That's about all there is," Tom told him. "Except that yesterday I rode over the pass Bannock way. There a Mexican kid over there herding sheep. The evening before someone had taken a shot at him from the timber near the mouth of Red Rock. He hightailed it, moved his sheep on out a mile or so. But that night after it was dark he went back up the cañon to have a look around. Claims he saw a bunch of about fifty head of cattle being driven out of Red Rock and across the flats."

Tom thumbed a match alight and touched it to his smoke, eyeing Ed Tolliver obliquely, not wanting to look at Sandy. But it was Sandy who said quietly: "Then you know they took the herd over the mountains by using one of those cañons on this side and then down Red Rock where the going's rocky?"

Tom tilted his head, adding: "That and the rain took care of sign."

"Did this kid see Bill Mathews?" Ed Tolliver asked.

The grating quality of the old man's words made Tom hesitate in his reply. But finally, stubbornly he decided to tell only the truth. "He saw three men. One could have been Matthews."

He was all at once feeling his hunger and tiredness and turned to the door now to pull on his poncho while behind him Ed Tolliver asked: "What're you going to do about it?"

"I've already written down into New Mexico to find out more about this partner of Stringfellow's."

"Meantime, we sit around twiddling our thumbs while we're rustled poor."

Tom's glance came around and he drawled: "What would you do, Ed? Lock Matthews up and lay yourself wide open for a false arrest charge?"

"I'd damn' well do something."

"I am doing it."

"Like hell. If you'd been on your toes, this. . . ."

"Ed," Sandy interrupted, "can't you understand that Tom's trying?"

"Trying! He was warming the seat of his pants when those cattle were driven off, wasn't he?" the oldster exploded. "What do we hire him for? To make guesses? To take pictures of dead men? To take a kid's word for something that may mean a man's neck?"

Tom was at the door now, realizing how futile it was to argue with the oldster. "OK, Ed," he said mildly, "I'm in the wrong. Forget what I said." And he opened the door.

He ignored the other's fresh tirade on his way out, not even listening to it. And the brief glance he gave Sandy showed him an expression of bafflement and contrition written on her face. She was pleading with her uncle as Tom closed the door.

All the way through his meal in the restaurant across the street Tom was thinking of Sandy, hardly tasting the steak and coffee he wolfed down. Never before had his thoughts of her been so confused, and now that circumstance had brought her so close to the troubles of his office he found a strange new bitterness blended with the long-felt hopelessness any thought of her invariably stirred in him.

He was paying for his meal when he heard the street door open. His mind still on Sandy, he was startled to hear her voice say behind him: "Tom, can I see you a moment?"

He wheeled around to see her standing there, a plaid cape about her shoulders and bare-headed, droplets of the misty rain silvering the wavy goldenness of her hair. She had a breathless, frightened look that at once made him reach his hat and poncho down off the wall and follow her through the door.

They were barely on the walk when she said in a tight voice: "Tom, something's happened. I'm terribly afraid."

"Ed?"

She nodded, looking up at him beseechingly. "I've never seen him this way. After you'd gone he had another of his attacks. Only this time he wouldn't let me get the doctor. Sick as he is, he thinks you're trying to blame this all on Phil."

"And do you?"

"No, Tom. Never." A wave of thankfulness ran through him

74

as she hurriedly went on: "But now he's gone. And I'm afraid, Tom, afraid it'll kill him."

"Gone where?"

"Out to see Phil, to try and get the truth from him. He wouldn't listen to me even when I reminded him the doctor had said he shouldn't ride."

Buckling his poncho, Tom said quietly: "Go on out to the house and wait. I'll bring him back."

The warmth and tenderness he remembered so well were in her dark eyes now as she looked up, saying softly, gravely: "Even after the way he's treated you, you can do this for him?"

"For you, Sandy," he told her. Then, thinking he was betraying too much of his feelings, he added: "For you and Phil."

Before he quite realized it, she had come close and, all at once tilting her head up, brushed his cheek with her lips. "Thank you, Tom," she said, and stepped on past him up the walk.

The old nearly forgotten excitement was quickening in him as he turned and watched the shadows swallow her slender shape. Yet as he started on toward the livery, his bitterness was like a dull knife pushing slowly to the innermost part of him. For he knew that the mention of Phil Kirby was really what had prompted Sandy's kiss.

II

He was four miles out the trail leading to Bit when the rain settled in again with a steady murmur rising over the hoof falls of the hired mare. The animal was hard-mouthed and had a rough jog, so that he was alternately running and walking her, trying to make time.

His thinking was as muddled as it had ever been, and he found he resented Ed Tolliver's uncalled-for contrariness more than he did the public opinion it might bring against him. He'd counted Ed as one of his friends and even the knowledge that the man was sick didn't ease his resentment over what was happening tonight. The old printer might easily put him back even what few steps he had taken in groping his way through the maze of this mysterious rustling, and now all he could put any faith in was Phil Kirby's common sense. If Kirby could see beyond Ed Tolliver's anger tonight, far enough beyond it to realize that his foreman, Matthews, needed watching, then perhaps everything would work out all right.

He had left the lower foothills and was rimming the wide cañon close below Bit's headquarters when all at once the mare's head lifted and a sound rose over her muffled, walking hoof strikes. Instinct made him swing a few feet off the trail before he reined in to listen. At once he caught the sound again—a strange, hoarse *rattling,* as though of a man gagging for breath.

Suddenly he realized that was exactly what he was hearing and an instant later he made out the faint black silhouette of a horse standing ahead of him in the trail. He reached inside his poncho and drew the .44 Colt from his thigh, swung quickly aground. Then, as quietly as he could, he walked in on the horse he now could see was riderless. As he moved, the sound strengthened with an eeriness that coolly needled the nerves along his back.

Gradually he picked out the detail of the horse that was now watching him. For a moment he didn't understand the shadowed line that ran down from the animal's near stirrup. The next he knew what it was, and, lowering the gun to his side, he ran in on the horse. His abrupt move frightened the animal and it shied a few feet farther along the trail, dragging whatever was caught in the stirrup.

"Whoa, boy. Easy," Tom drawled, walking on slowly now.

He knew even before he looked down at the figure the horse

was dragging that it must be Ed Tolliver. Gently, speaking to the horse as he closed in, he finally pulled the oldster's boot free of the stirrup. He knelt in the mud, laying the Colt aside as the horse walked away. And now he had to lean down to catch the faint sound of Ed's breathing that had moments ago rasped so loudly.

"Ed, it's Tom," he said gently. "Can you hear?"

He thought he saw Ed Tolliver's eyes open but wasn't sure until the man mumbled feebly: "Tom, you guessed . . . guessed wrong . . . We had it out . . . and . . . and. . . ."

The words trailed off with a terrible finality as Tom was trying to picture what had happened. The oldster, already having suffered one heart attack tonight, had evidently had another as the result of a violent argument with someone at Bit, Bill Matthews probably.

Cradling Ed's head and shoulders gently in the bend of one arm now, he lifted the man's limp upper body clear of the mud, drawling: "Rest a bit and we'll go on home, Ed." Then he asked: "Who was it you talked to? Matthews?"

Although he bent low, his ear close to the printer's mouth, the only sound that reached him was the steady drone of the rain.

All at once alarmed, he ran his free hand in under the other's poncho, feeling of the flat chest. There was no heartbeat. Ed Tolliver was dead.

Tom knelt there with the heaviness of regret settling through him. For a moment he wondered what share he'd had in killing the old man. Thinking it through, he was finally convinced that nothing he had done could have been avoided.

Then he got to thinking of something else, of Ed's last words and their meaning. He could still hear the faint voice, catch its every intonation. And at once he was asking himself what Ed had meant in saying that Tom had guessed wrong. And who had he been speaking of when he said *we?*

Now a slow excitement was stirring in him over a startling possibility. He had guessed wrong, Ed had said. The only guess he had made had been on Matthews. A contrary reasoning was making him ask himself if it could have been Phil Kirby, and not Matthews, who had "had it out" with Ed at Bit tonight. Dispassionately, not wanting to be biased by the fact that Kirby was the man of Sandy's choosing, he looked back upon several things that had long puzzled him about Bit's new owner. Why, for instance, did Kirby never mention his past? And why, when Kirby could have kept Bit's old foreman on after he bought the brand, did he bring in a complete stranger like Matthews who in less then a year had gained the reputation of having mismanaged the outfit? Where did Kirby's money come from, money that had let him build a big new house of square-hewn logs and buy out his neighbor higher in the hills at a price everyone thought was considerably more than the land was worth? Did it mean anything that this newly bought range give access to the high country that dropped directly into Red Rock Cañon on the far side of the mountains? All these unanswered questions could be tied in with Ed Tolliver's dying mention of a wrong guess. Or could they?

Finally, his mind weary of trying to read what lay behind the printer's last words, Tom reached down and started to unbuckle the dead man's poncho, intending to wrap the body in it, rope it to the horse standing nearby, and head for town.

Suddenly his hands went motionless. His glance dropped to the dead man's shadowed face again. And, wonderingly, he breathed: "Would you let me, Ed? It wouldn't hurt. And it might help."

He sat there for long seconds, feeling he should discard the reckless notion that had struck him. But, try as he would to rule it out, it kept nagging at him.

Reluctantly almost, he reached out and picked up the Colt finally. Coming slowly erect, he stood a moment staring down at the body. Then he softly drawled: "We'll lay our bets, Ed, you and me."

He lifted the Colt slightly and lined it at Ed Tolliver's chest, thumbing back the hammer. After the weapon pounded against his hand, the second roar of the explosion racketed back from the nearby rim in a hollow roll of sound.

Quickly then, because Bit headquarters lay only a quarter mile away, Tom Marolt went over to his horse and swung up into the saddle.

He didn't take the trail going away but cut on over for the timber.

III

The next day, bright and cloudless, was as confused as any day had ever been for Tom Marolt, the apparent aimlessness of developments doing little to ease the tightness of his nerves.

Last night's long talk with Sandy paid a dividend early in the morning when she came to the office with her neighbor, George Collyer. Tom listened to what they had to say, at length telling Sandy: "If he rode out to Bit that late, chances are he spent the night with Phil. He'll turn up. Why worry?"

"But I am worried," she said, and he marveled at her capacity for acting when she knew it was all a sham. "There's a lot of work at the shop and he should be there. This isn't like him."

"Want us to go look for him?" Tom asked her.

As she hesitated, Collyer offered: "There's a couple things I could be doing out that way. If you can wait till afternoon to know about Ed, I'll just swing up to Bit and have a look. Now I wouldn't fret, Sandy."

So it was settled that way and Sandy and Collyer left.

Shortly after 11:00 Tom was called out by Simmons, owner

of the Mercantile, to ride up Alder Basin and serve a dispossess notice on a family that had moved uninvited onto Simmons's homestead. He didn't get back to town until nearly 2:00, hoping that by then something would have developed according to his plan of last night. But nothing had. There was no one in his office, not even Collyer, and it tried his patience to go about his duties as though everything was as it should be.

At 3:00 p.m. he went to the post office and waited for the mail off the Burnt Creek stage to be sorted, afterward idling back up the street with it under his arm. He was looking through the letters as he turned into his office to find Sandy and Collyer waiting for him.

"Tom, something's happened," Sandy said at once. She looked at Collyer, her voice breaking quite convincingly as she asked: "Could you tell him, George?"

"It looks bad, Sheriff," Collyer said with great gravity. "Kirby says Ed was out there last night and left around ten, headed for home."

Tom eyed him quizzically. "What else?"

Collyer shook his head. "That's all there is. Ed's just plain disappeared."

After a proper show of surprise Tom drawled: "Kirby couldn't give you anything to go on?"

"Only that Ed had complained of his heart."

"Then, if anything happened to him on the way into town, we ought to find him somewhere between there and here."

Collyer nodded. "So Kirby said. He rode most of the way to town with me, him to one side of the trail, me to the other. We didn't find a thing, not even a track. That rain washed the ground clean as a whistle. Now Kirby's gone back to gather up his crew and put 'em out along those other trails this side of Bit. He thinks maybe Ed got lost."

"Hardly likely," Tom said, looking at Sandy.

There was a dazed, questioning look in her eyes that made Collyer say awkwardly: "Well, I'll be gettin' on. Anything I can do, Sheriff?"

"You might spread the word around, George," Tom told him, glancing at the clock above his desk. "We'll all meet at the livery, say at four. Better figure on spending the night out, so it'll be grub and blankets."

"I'll look after it." Collyer touched his hat to Sandy and was gone.

The door had barely closed behind him when Sandy breathed: "You were right, Tom."

"About what?"

"About their moving the . . . moving Uncle Ed." She paused, uncertainty and a strong sadness in her. Then her look became pleading. "Tom, everything's gone so wrong. Would you tell me again what you said last night? How they'd move Uncle Ed's body. Tell me again what that will mean."

"It may prove whether Matthews is innocent or guilty. If he's our rustler, he'll do anything to keep us from finding Ed's body near Bit. He'll figure we might start watching the outfit, which would spoil his game. So even if he hasn't a prayer of knowing who shot Ed, he'll make sure the body isn't found where it can hurt him."

Sandy was frowning now, obviously not understanding. "But what you're saying can hold true of Phil, too, Tom. How can you be sure that it was Matthews who found Ed?"

"That's a chance I'm taking," he told her uncomfortably. "They had to hear that shot last night, didn't they? It was raining, and Kirby, if he got curious, would naturally send the crew out to see what it was rather than go himself. Matthews would be plenty sure he was the first man down that trail . . . if he's guilty."

His explanation seemed to satisfy her and for a few moments

neither of them said anything. But gradually over that interval Tom's rising hopes of having put her off faded. For her look became a questioning one once more and presently she said: "Collyer didn't say that Phil had mentioned a shot. Yet Phil must have heard it. Could it . . . could it possibly mean that Phil's dishonest?"

"No such thing," he insisted stubbornly, although he was having to force himself to sound convincing.

He wondered if he had been wrong in telling her only a half truth last night when, repeating Ed's last words, he had omitted any mention of her uncle saying he had made a wrong guess. Because he wasn't dead sure of Ed's meaning himself, he had decided not to worry her with the enigma. She knew everything else, that Ed had argued with someone at Bit, that he had died there on the trail of a heart attack, that Tom had put a bullet in the body. Now, for the second time, he was explaining why he had fired that bullet.

"Last night you were counting on Matthews's hiding the body, Tom. Do you really think that's what happened?"

"I do. There wouldn't have been much time for him to do anything right away. He was probably the first man down the trail and my guess is he carried Ed off the trail into some brush, then got rid of the horse. Later, after everyone had turned in, he'd have come back and packed Ed away somewhere, plenty far away. I . . . I warned you we were playing long odds, Sandy."

"I know, I know," she said miserably, going to the window and staring out over the street. "And I also know, as you did, that Ed would have wanted us to do this if it will help. But, Tom, I'm not so . . . not so sure of Phil any longer."

He was thankful that her back was turned, that she couldn't read his look. "Don't lay any bets against Phil Kirby," he told her. "He's a good man, one of the best."

She had nothing to say to that. And now, feeling ill at ease, he looked at his mail again, thumbing through the envelopes that he could see were mostly Reward or election notices.

Suddenly he gave a start, staring down at a long official-looking envelope. In its upper corner was a return address: *U.S. Commissioner's Office, Santa Fé, Territory of New Mexico.*

He glanced quickly at Sandy, saw that her back was still turned, and tore open the envelope. He read:

Dear Sheriff Marolt:

It looks like you are onto something up there. Ted Stringfellow's partner was as you describe your man. Here is something more to go on. His real name is William Matthews Ives, which ties in with the handle he is now using. He is wanted along with Stringfellow for carving up some Mexicans in a saloon brawl down in Las Cruces.

If you arrest Ives, you can notify the sheriff at Las Cruces. Until your letter arrived, I had been hoping this matter might help me locate The Duke. In case you have never heard of The Duke, he was the brains behind a stage robbery that cost a bullion shipper $40,000 and involved the mails. Stringfellow, and possibly Ives, were thought to have worked with him, but there was no proof against them.

So it looks like you have all the luck this time and that I have been working a cold trail.

Y'rs obediently,
Cyrus Quillan

"What is it, Tom?"

Those words knifed through Tom's complete absorption, and, his glance lifting, he found Sandy staring at him. He hastily stuffed the letter back in its envelope, tossing it to his desk with the rest of the mail, drawling: "Not a thing, Sandy."

She came across and looked down at the desk. "You looked so funny, Tom. Almost frightened." She reached down and picked up the envelope, then looked questioningly at him. "From Santa Fé. Is it the word you were waiting for? News of Matthews?"

There was a point beyond which he couldn't go in deceiving her as he nodded, hoping her curiosity would be satisfied.

But it wasn't, for she said with a sure intuition: "It says something you don't want me to know, doesn't it?"

"Now look, Sandy, I. . . ."

"Doesn't it, Tom?" Then, when he gave her no answer: "Are you afraid because of what I'll think of Phil's hiring such a man?"

"Not exactly. There is just no use in bothering you with it."

She regarded him steadily a moment. Then in a low voice she asked: "Would you let me read it, Tom? I've got to know everything. Remember, Uncle Ed is dead. He's been a father to me for ten years. Isn't it my right to know anything that has to do with him?"

He drew in a deep sigh. "You can read it, Sandy."

She took the sheet from the envelope and he stood watching her, the seconds dragging interminably and a feeling of helplessness and self-loathing gripping him. When at last she laid the letter on his desk and turned to stare at him in an oddly puzzled way, he had a wild hope that made him say: "See, it's nothing we didn't know already. Matthews must have had Stringfellow on the outside, helping him. Maybe they fell out and Matthews got rid of him by rushing him off that rim trail up Dry Creek. Or maybe it was an accident. Anyway, I've got enough to go on now to make the arrest."

"Yes, you have," she murmured. A vast relief was flowing through him when all at once her expression changed to a wide-eyed wonderment and she breathed—"Tom."—in a hushed, awed voice. In an instant he knew with a numbing certainty that the realization of what she had so far missed reading into the letter had come to her: "That other man, The Duke," she said, "he could be Phil."

"You're not thinking straight, Sandy!" His voice grated with a real anger.

"That's why you looked that way," she went on, ignoring his protest. "You . . . it's what you were thinking, too."

From somewhere deep inside him he found the calmness and level-headedness to say: "You can't mean that. How could it be? Phil Kirby's been straight as a string. That letter doesn't say a thing we could hold against him. Except that he made the mistake of hiring a wanted man."

"It says there was a third man, Tom. One who's wanted for robbery."

He nodded. "So it does. But it doesn't describe him or give us a thing to go on. So why pick on Phil?"

His probing glance didn't miss an iota of change in her expression, for suddenly it had become the most important chore he had ever tackled to keep his spoken opinions strictly neutral, to let Sandy decide this thing for herself. He had his own conviction, based on Ed Tolliver's dying words and now on this letter. Yet something far more important than Phil Kirby's guilt or innocence hung in the balance now, something so deeply personal that the outcome of the next few moments could either make him a whole man again or add immeasurably to the burden of his depression and bitterness.

Sandy's look had gone wholly serious. She seemed to realize the importance of this moment as she said quietly: "There have been things about Phil I've never understood until just now. He never talks of home, of a mother or a father. Then there's his money. He's never said where it came from. A man who's asked a girl to marry him wouldn't hide these things from her unless he had a reason."

"You've probably never asked him about them, Sandy."

"There's another thing." He could no more read a meaning into those irrelevant words than he could understand the way her eyes were filling with tears, or their tender regard of him. She shook her head. "No, it's not that, Tom. It's because one of the few times I can remember ever seeing Phil really angry was because of you." When he didn't say anything, she went on: "It seems I was talking about you too much. He wanted to know why I compared everything he did to the way you'd do it. Of course, I hadn't realized that I'd mentioned you so often."

He was confused now, not wanting to listen to a small voice in him that told him things were far different than he had been seeing them. He was groping for words, still trying to find a way of defending Phil Kirby against her accusations when sounds from street caught his attention.

Sandy looked toward the window. "What can that be?"

The increasing pitch of excited voices from down the street took him across to the window and at that moment they caught the sound of hurried steps coming along the walk. Someone ran past the window and a second later the door swung open on George Collyer.

"They've found him, Sheriff!" Collyer said, seeing Tom standing there. "He was shot! Kirby's on his way here with him and. . . ."

He saw Sandy then and his words broke off. He stood there embarrassed and confused until she said: "It's all right, George. I had to know it sooner or later."

Collyer said haltingly: "We . . . we're all sorry as can be, Sandy." Then he added ominously: "The man that did it won't live much longer than it takes us to track him down."

Tom realized that he and Sandy still had a part to play and he said gravely: "George is right, Sandy. We've all lost a good friend. We'll do what we can to square things for Ed." He nodded to the door. "Can I take you up to the house?"

"No, Tom, I'll stay here."

He stepped out the door, looking along the street to see a knot of men coming slowly up this near walk toward the jail. The talking and shouting was over now as they soberly eyed the street. Out there Phil Kirby, astride a big sorrel and the rope of a led horse tied to his saddle horn, rode abreast the building immediately below and was already turning in to the jail's tie rail. The shape of the bulky tarp-wrapped object roped to the animal he led was the reason for the stern cast of the Bit owner's face as he shortly drew rein and swung aground.

"Does Sandy know?" were his first words after he had ducked under the rail and stepped onto the walk.

Tom nodded. "George told her. She's in here."

Kirby's glance shuttled to Collyer. "Would you take Ed on up to Lansing for me, George?"

Collyer went out onto the street at once, picking up the reins of Kirby's horse, and going astride the animal. Then he headed up the street in the direction of the feed mill, owned by the coroner.

"Ed was shot, according to George," Tom said. "Where did you find him?"

"Four miles out, beyond the forks to my place." Kirby was heading for the door. Within a stride of it he abruptly stopped, half turning to Tom: "You'd better get in here and listen to what I have to say, Tom."

Following the Bit man, Tom entered the office in time to see Kirby take Sandy gently in his arms. But her head was turned away from him, and Tom noticed that her fists were clenched and that she stood rigidly as Kirby told her grimly: "We'll settle the score for Ed, Sandy. If I'd only known six hours ago what I do now, it would already be settled."

She drew away from him. "What is it you know?"

Instead of answering her, he asked: "You knew Ed came out

to see me last night?"

"I did. So did Tom."

There was a coolness in her tone that seemed to puzzle Kirby. For, after studying her narrowly a moment, he looked quickly around at Tom and his tone lacked its usual smoothness as he told them: "Then you must know what he came to me about. I couldn't believe what he had to say about Matthews. He was sore, wanted me to do something right then. We swapped some pretty salty talk and Ed had one of his attacks. Not a bad one, mind you."

Tom, afraid that Kirby would be able to tell from the loathing in Sandy's eyes that something was wrong, drawled: "Sandy, you'd better go now. Phil and I will figure this out."

"I'm staying." There was a bluntness to her words that did the very thing Tom wanted least. Kirby's glance at once went to her and his eyes showed a definite wariness as he caught her expression.

"Sandy, this'll only make it harder for you." Tom spoke quietly but firmly. "Go on home and rest."

Kirby frowned, asking suspiciously: "What is this? Why shouldn't she stay?"

"You said you knew something," Sandy stated, the stare she fixed on Kirby openly furious. "Tell us what it is."

The Bit man was unsure of himself now. But he was also evidently unwilling to risk asking the reason for Sandy's strange antagonism, for shortly he said: "Matthews is gone. No one's seen him since eleven last night. That roan stallion is missing from the barn corral along with a new saddle I bought last week."

Sandy gave Tom a look that was baffled, imploring. And Tom hastened to speak before she could put any meaning to this unexpected development and say the wrong thing: "So you think Matthews killed Ed?"

Kirby nodded. "What else is there to think? It ties in with what Ed came to see me about. Matthews must have seen Ed ride in. He could have listened at a window, then followed Ed when he left."

"And no one heard anything? No shot?"

The Bit man's barely perceptible start told Tom all he needed to know. "We found Ed beyond the forks to my place," Kirby stated carefully. "How could we hear a shot from that far away?"

Tom saw that Sandy was about to say something and put in hastily: "Ed was shot within a quarter mile of your layout, Phil." He could see the effect of his words, for Kirby stiffened again and that heavy-lidded wariness showed once more in his eyes. Tom didn't give him time to steady himself, adding: "Matthews real name was Ives. He was a sidekick of that stranger they found below the rim up Dry Creek last spring. Ted Stringfellow was the stranger's name."

Quickly, too quickly Kirby asked: "How do you know all this?"

Tom nodded to the desk. "A letter from Santa Fé. It's right there behind you. Read it."

Kirby started to turn, hesitated. It was obvious that he wasn't risking putting his back to Tom. And now the wariness built higher in him as he said carefully: "Suppose you tell me what it says."

Tom saw that Sandy's hateful look had given way to a fearful, alarmed one now. Apprehension stabbed through him and he said: "Sandy, will you let me talk to Phil alone?"

She nodded mutely and started for the door. But as she passed Kirby, he suddenly reached out and caught her arm in a grip so hard that she winced.

"She'll stay," Kirby drawled. "Something's goin' on here I don't like." His glance flicked down to the .44 at Tom's waist, then lifted again. "What was in that letter, Sheriff?"

Tom's instinct a moment ago as Kirby stopped Sandy had been to draw his Colt and risk a shot before the odds went too heavily against him. But now, as Kirby pulled Sandy close to him, he knew that he had lost his small advantage. And that knowledge plus his knowing that Sandy was in real danger now struck him dumb.

Seeing him hesitate, Sandy said quietly: "Tell him, Tom. If you don't, I will."

There was a finality to her ultimatum that he couldn't ignore. Neither could he let her voice her suspicions of the Bit man. Finally, hoping there was still a way of getting her out of here, he drawled easily: "Why so spooky, Phil? It's only that we learned there was a third man tied in with Matthews. Sandy's been wanting me to tell you about him right away. I've tried to convince her I was to have a try at him on my own first."

Some of Kirby's suspicion seemed to fade then. Yet he didn't let go his hold on Sandy's arm as he asked: "Why didn't you want to tell me about this man?"

Tom lifted his shoulders tiredly. "For the same reason I'd hoped Ed wouldn't write that editorial. I've put in a lot of time on this rustling, Phil. I was beginning to get somewhere when that editorial blew the thing wide open. Now what's happened? Ed's dead because of it. Matthews has disappeared. Can you blame me if I want to go at it on my own?"

A look of relief, of near belief, was on Kirby's face now and he let Sandy's arm go, saying: "Sorry I did that, Sandy. But you two were actin' plenty queer for such a penny-ante reason. Tom, last night I told you to count on me. I'll say it again. I want to help any way I can. Now is there anything you can tell me about this third man?"

A vast relief flowed through Tom as he saw Sandy backing away from Kirby. He nodded, to hold the Bit man's attention, drawling: "Whoever he is, he must have helped Matthews move

Ed's body last night. I can even make another guess. Matthews is probably dead."

Kirby's surprise was genuine as he breathed: "No."

Again Tom nodded, speaking hurriedly so that Kirby wouldn't notice Sandy. "This other man's been the brains behind the deal. The only thing he hadn't counted on was Ed's dying the way he did, so close to Bit. He had to move fast, had to get rid of Ed's body, then take care of Matthews. Maybe Matthews lost his nerve, or maybe this third man decided Matthews might give him away. Who knows? Anyway, that's the way I've figured it."

Kirby tried to look baffled, yet neither his look nor his shake of the head was convincing. He glanced Sandy's way abruptly, and for the first time aware that she was no longer within his reach, his eyes whipped warily around at Tom again. He didn't really want to ask what he did then, yet curiosity and uncertainty drove him to it: "Who is this third man?"

Tom deliberately considered his reply, knowing that it was futile to speak to Sandy again about leaving, knowing also with a dismal certainty that he would never have a better chance at Kirby than he had right now.

"You really want to know?" he asked tonelessly.

"I do."

"It's you. You're the third man, The Duke."

Even before his words were out, Kirby's right hand drove upward and under his coat toward the Colt Tom knew he always wore there in a shoulder holster. And as he moved, Tom lunged in.

That stark fear over what might happen to Sandy made Tom's move lightning-fast. He was quick enough, as his shoulder smashed against Kirby's chest, to wrap his arms around the man and pin that right hand beneath the coat, driving Kirby backward and slamming him against the wall.

Kirby's left knee lifted hard, catching him in the groin. For an instant Tom's hold loosened as they thrashed away from the wall and staggered across toward the window. Sandy cried out unintelligibly and that sound steeled Tom against the pain, made him bury his head in Kirby's chest and hug the man with a vice-like hold. He could feel the Colt clear of its holster now and knew that relaxing his hold for even a fraction of a second would mean he was to die.

He put all the drive he could in his legs, crowding Kirby backward, never letting him get his balance. Kirby's snarl of rage only gave him added strength. All at once he felt Kirby jolt hard against something. Then the Bit man was falling backward, dragging him with him. There came the *jangle* of breaking glass. Tom felt a jagged edge of it tear at his shoulder and knew they were falling through the window. Then the wind was driven from Kirby in a sharp groan as they crashed down onto the walk outside, Kirby underneath.

At that instant a hard blow struck Tom in the chest and an explosion deafened him. He felt a muscle spasm shudder through Kirby's body, so strong that it broke his hold. The Bit man gave a choked gasp. Suddenly every muscle in him went loose. Thinking it a trick, Tom tightened his hold. Then he heard a step on the walk close by and someone touched him on the shoulder. He looked up. George Collyer was standing over him, his look awed as he said soberly: "I think he's dead, Sheriff."

Tom saw the office door swing open, saw Sandy come out onto the walk. For an instant she stood, pale and staring at him in wide-eyed terror. Then, as he pulled his arms from under Kirby and rushed up to a sitting position astride the man, an expression of wonderment and gladness crossed the girl's face and she ran out to him. She knelt there beside him. Vaguely, as he took her in his arms, Tom was aware of men running this way along the walk. Then he forgot everything but the girl who clung to him, trembling with her emotion.

"It's all right now, Sandy," he told her.

Ever so softly, as her head lifted, she said: "Tom, its been so . . . we've been away from each other so long." And their lips met to seal the promise of her words.

★ ★ ★ ★ ★

DOC GENTRY

★ ★ ★ ★ ★

This story was completed in late November, 1936. Jon Glidden's agent submitted it to Popular Publications and it was bought for $67.50 on January 26, 1937. Trying to get in the spirit of titling stories that would please pulp magazine editors, the author's title for the story was "Doc Gentry's Gun-Cub." That title was changed to "A Button Sides a Saw-Bones" when it appeared in *Ace-High Magazine* (3/37). For its appearance here the author's title has been abbreviated.

It was a blunt slug from Clyde Neal's .45 that made a cripple of strapping young Joe Egan. There was no vicious intent behind the wild drunken shot that Neal whipped at the whirling feet of a terrorized percentage girl in the Nugget Saloon. He and a half dozen of his Wagon Hammer riders were only whooping it up—having a roaring good time. Neal was just a little careless or the bullet would not have ricocheted in that high piercing *whine* through the swing doors, to be prolonged by Joe's scream as it whipped into his spine.

That drawn-out wail of the stricken boy instantly smothered the uproarious din in the Nugget. By the time eight or ten of the more sober citizens had swarmed out through the doors and onto the half-lighted walk, Doc Gentry was already kneeling beside the prostrate form. Lucky for Joe Egan that the sawbones was across the street when it happened; otherwise, someone would have tried to move him and it would have been fatal.

The first thing Doc Gentry said as he straightened from his hasty examination was: "Keep back, you knot heads! And don't touch him. Get me some boiling water and clean towels." He glanced around the circle of faces, picked out one of them. "Sam, you run like hell to my office and bring me my black bag off the desk."

Back in the Nugget, at the center table, Clyde Neal listened a minute to the excited voices before he dropped his pearl-handled Colt into its tooled-leather holster and mumbled thickly: "Some damn' kid. Why the hell do they hang around a place like this?" He pushed his cards into the center of the table, growling: "Deal another hand, Horse Collar."

Doc Gentry performed the operation there on the boardwalk, by the light of an oil lantern, and the one who handed him his instruments and bandages was the very girl whose dancing feet Clyde Neal's bullet had so narrowly missed. Her eyes were moist with tears and the cold cut through her flimsy dress, but she stuck it out. After Gentry had tied the last bandage and washed the blood from his hands, he looked up at her and said: "You've got guts, sister."

They laid the twelve-year-old boy on a stretcher made from two coats and a pair of broom handles and carried him home. Gentry walked alongside Joe, cursing the whole way. Cursing, first, Clyde Neal, and then the man carrying the front end of the stretcher because he stumbled once. But they got Joe to the Egan shack alive and put him to bed.

Joe's mother, Sarah Egan, hid her grief until the others had gone and only Gentry remained. It was then she broke down, her fine face giving way to the spasms of grief she had so far held in check. Gentry hid his embarrassment by taking her in his arms and letting her sob quietly on his shoulder. Once he lowered his head until her fine chestnut hair caressed his cheek, but he drew away quickly, as though he had taken advantage of her helplessness.

"He'll pull through," he murmured, trying to sound convincing.

Oddly enough he was not thinking of Joe just then. He was thinking of Sarah Egan. What was going to happen to her now that Joe could no longer bring home the $3 a week George Tade paid him for helping at the hardware store. And just where in hell was Paul Egan, that worthless, wandering good-for-nothing who thought he could better support a wife and boy by prospecting in the hills than by drawing his $40 a month punching cattle?

Gentry left the shack as soon as he could, telling Sarah he would be back, asking her to see that Joe lay quietly if he regained consciousness. He walked up the alley and straight to his office. There he took a worn Smith and Wesson .45 from the drawer of his roll-top desk.

In the orange glow of the lamp his lean face took on the look of a man of fifty even though he was a good fifteen years younger than that. He was meticulous as he oiled the gun, wiped it clean, tested the action. Then, satisfied, he reloaded it and blew out the lamp and went down the street.

He turned in at the Nugget Saloon.

The smoke-fogged room was quiet now, except for the group that sat with Clyde Neal at the poker table. Sheriff Bill Troutman idled at the bar in an all too obvious state of alcoholic apathy. There was no sense in calling on him at a time like this. He was Clyde Neal's man anyway. Six Wagon Hammer riders stood or lounged in chairs about the poker table, watching the five in the game. Two half empty quart bottles of whiskey were near the rim of the table in the litter of cigarette ashes, shot glasses, and spilled tobacco.

Clyde Neal's chips were strewn in disorder on the table before him. His shaggy brows were raised, wrinkling his forehead, as though he found it an effort to keep his eyes focused on the cards he held in his broad fist. Neither he nor the others at the game noticed Doc Gentry's approach—did not, in fact, even see him until they felt the sudden silence over the rest of the room that left their own voices sounding loudly in their ears.

When they looked up, Gentry was standing close to the table, close enough so that the fan spread of light from the shaded lamp above cut a clean swath of orange across his thighs. From across the board Clyde Neal raised his liquor-dulled eyes to see what was happening. He met Doc Gentry's measuring glance and caught the glitter in the doctor's slate-gray eyes. A man would have had the time to count to ten, slowly, before Gentry, began to speak: "Neal, ever since I came to this country, I've been digging Wagon Hammer lead . . . mostly yours . . . out of people. Tonight I dug one of your slugs out of Sarah Egan's boy. Since no one else here has the guts to cut you in two, I'm delegating myself. You can go for your iron any time."

Gentry's hands were hanging at his sides as he spoke, but now every eye caught the unfamiliar bulge of a gun butt beneath his coat. He took one backward step, kicked a chair out of the way, and stood there waiting, watching.

Neal's swarthy handsome face took on its most engaging smile, yet his black eyes belied the expression. They were blank, cloudy, as he moved to rise slowly from his chair. His hand dropped swiftly before he had fully straightened.

It was incredible to those who watched—incredible that Doc Gentry's hand could move with that swift practiced smoothness. Horse Collar Kearney, the Wagon Hammer ramrod, lunged as the two men started to move. Yet for all his speed, Kearney had barely time to strike up Gentry's arm before the .45 splintered the silence with its roar.

Luckily Kearney's blow pushed Gentry off balance, for the next instant Clyde Neal's Colt added to the gun blast and his slug tore a hole in Gentry's right coat sleeve. Drunk or sober, Neal could shoot.

Horse Collar struck again, before Gentry could recover his balance, and his blow connected. Gentry's knees gave way and he pitched forward onto the floor, half under the table. . . .

It was over a half minute later. Two quick-thinking onlookers grappled with Neal and succeeded in tearing his weapon out of his hand. Others hastily picked Gentry up off the floor and carried him out. Neal yelled for his gun, cursing the men who held him, threatening to gun-whip the lot of them when they let him go. It was again Horse Collar who saved the situation by going over behind the bar and returning with a dipper of water that he threw in Neal's face. Of all the men there, Horse Collar was the only one who could have done that to Neal and still lived.

After that, the Wagon Hammer boss quieted down. He asked rather sheepishly for his six-gun but made no remonstrance when Kearney refused to give it to him. He took a long pull at the bottle before they took him away and hoisted him into his saddle. Kearney had to tie him into it before he rounded up his other eight riders and headed out of town. Neal was like a baby in Kearney's hands when drunk. For five years now Horse Collar had nursed him through these drunken sprees.

Doc Gentry thanked Horse Collar Kearney for what he had done the next time he saw him, a week later. By that time Gentry had thought it over. The soreness from Kearney's blow had gone from his jaw; by that time, too, he knew that Joe Egan was going to live, and he felt better about things.

Horse Collar nodded soberly and said: "The boss wanted me to settle up Joe's bill, Doc."

"Bill, hell!" Gentry roared. "Joe Egan's left leg is paralyzed. If Clyde's good at making new legs for a twelve-year-old, I'll put him to work. Unless he is, keep him away from me." He paused a moment, looking fixedly at Kearney. "Horse Collar, why don't you break away from that outfit?"

Kearney shrugged and said mysteriously: "You don't know where else I could make decent money, do you, Doc?"

Doc wanted to tell him that no man had ever made decent money, clean money, working for the Wagon Hammer, but he didn't, because he had a kind of wry affection for Horse Collar. Nevertheless, he knew that Clyde Neal raised cattle much the same as he did alfalfa—several crops a year—and knew, too, that Horse Collar tolerated it because of the good money Neal paid him. There were ranchers across the hills who could have prevented the loss of their prime beef each year if they had organized and ridden over to the Wagon Hammer to shoot it out for what was rightfully theirs. They didn't, and, because they didn't, the Wagon Hammer prospered accordingly.

It was a month before Doc Gentry received word in a roundabout way that Doc Swain from Rimrock City was now being called to patch bullet holes for the Wagon Hammer, instead of himself. And the same day he learned that Sarah Egan's husband had been found dead in a drifted gulch up above Virginia City. Death was due to exposure and alcoholic poisoning.

He thought: *That means I'll have to take care of her and Joe. And there'll be no Wagon Hammer doctor bills to help me out. Hell!* And right then, Doc admitted that he loved Sarah.

Joe Egan was husky for a boy of twelve. Six weeks after the accident he was getting around pretty well on a crutch, as well as he would ever be unless Gentry found a way of bringing in a specialist from San Francisco.

The day after Gentry bought Al Bennet's old sorrel mare for Joe, he helped the boy to saddle early in the afternoon. Joe was going out after a rabbit.

"Get going, kid," Doc said. "Bring home two and I'll come over and help you and your mom eat 'em."

Joe rode off, taking the west trail out of town. The air was chill, yet the motion of the mare and the sun's warmth kept him comfortable. To either side of him the abrupt rocky upslope of the piñon-dotted hills looked inviting, but he knew that there would be better hunting farther on.

Just before he rode between the two high shoulders that

formed the bottleneck of the gulch, he overtook Pay Dirt Warren. Pay Dirt was patiently plodding along beside his one loaded burro, his foot-long beard lying down over his chest outside his buckskin coat. No one knew how many years Pay Dirt had been in these hills, nor did they know where he panned the dust he brought into town with him six or eight times each year. There were a few who had tried to find out, hiding up by his shack in the hills, but they swore Pay Dirt spent the whole time sleeping, that he never stirred from his cabin.

Joe hailed him as he rode past on the trail, knowing, as anyone else in Bottle Gulch should have known, that Pay Dirt's greeting, if any, would be nothing beyond a curt nod. To him, silent old Warren's brief jerk of the head was ample recognition, so he rode on, feeling very good indeed.

Immediately beyond the hills he cut off across a rocky stretch to the north and put the mare in a swinging canter. A little less than a mile ahead was that winding, choked line of brush marking where the river came down out of the hills. There he would find rabbits. He picked out his favorite spot and rode to it. It lay fifty yards below the wooden bridge where the trail cut across the river and swung north to the hills, toward Rimrock City.

Joe was surprised to find the brush so thick, but then he remembered that the summer before had been a wet one. He gave up the idea of hunting from the saddle and headed the mare toward the three big cottonwoods that grew close to the bridge.

Above the racket the mare's hoofs made, Joe heard a rabbit scurry off behind him. He turned, saw the rabbit disappear too late to offer a shot, but his glance took in Pay Dirt Warren and his burro emerging, just then, from behind the hill on the trail.

Joe had drawn rein under the cottonwoods, and was reaching down to lift his crutch from the saddle boot when he heard the shots. They were close, and the four of them made an uneven, low-throated *booming* that slapped the echoes back from the hills two seconds later. Joe would not have thought much of it if he had not heard, five seconds later, the distant pounding of hoofs, the *rattle* of heavy wheels, and the shouts.

Instantly wary, he piled out of the saddle as best he could. From here he could not look across the river and up the trail, but he could hear the horses pounding nearer, the *rattle* of doubletree chains. He got his crutch, took the reins in his hands, and hobbled quickly over to get a look up the trail.

The instant it came into view he drew quickly back again. For down it, coming hell-for-leather, boiled the stage with Frank Semple holding the reins and whipping the team for all he was worth. Behind the stage, strung out in an uneven line, came five riders. All five wore bandannas bound about their faces. Joe saw two of them pull in a little and whip out three shots at the stage, saw the blue powder smoke as it puffed from their six-guns and faded out behind them.

Frank Semple dropped the reins, came to his feet clawing his chest, and fell forward and down. The heavy front wheel on the offside of the lumbering vehicle bounced a little as it ran over Semple, and the horses, feeling the slack on the reins, slowed to a trot, and then to a walk.

As the masked riders slid their broncos one by one to a quick stop beside the stagecoach, Joe saw the door open. The coach's one passenger started to climb down the step with hands high above his head. The low-throated snort of a .45 greeted him; he went suddenly loose, missed his footing, and half somersaulted to the ground to lie still.

Joe reached back to clamp his hand over his mare's nostrils to stop her from nickering, then he crawled back until he had to stoop down and look out from under the cottonwood branches to see what was going on. Here the brush and trees effectively hid him. He was frightened so badly that his teeth chattered and a slow paralysis seemed to stiffen his muscles.

He saw one of the riders climb up into the seat of the stage while another dismounted and went up to the lead team and held them by the reins. The man on the seat lifted the lid of the boot, heaved out three heavy bags, and let them fall to the ground before he climbed down again.

The five of them worked fast. They picked up Frank Semple and heaved him into the coach. He was dead; Joe could tell by his horrible limpness as they swung him in through the door. The man lying beside the stage was picked up and thrown in with Frank. Then, with a deliberateness that brought a slow nausea to Joe's vitals, the horses were cut from the traces while two men pulled loose some upholstery on the inside and set it afire. In less than a minute the flames licked up and made a raging pyre of the coach.

Things moved with such stunning rapidity that Joe Egan did not see Pay Dirt Warren until Pay Dirt had almost reached the bridge. He wanted to shout a warning, but that would have cost him his own life, so he remained silent, thinking suddenly how odd it was that no one paid any attention to the old prospector.

The next instant he saw the reason. As though they had accomplished their purpose, the five masked riders swung to their saddles and rode toward the bridge, toward Pay Dirt. He made no move to get out of their way; in fact, it was as though he could not see the men who were almost on him. He held his plodding stride until he gained the wooden planks of the bridge. There he stopped and waited.

All five of the riders rode onto the bridge at the other end. Then, unbelievably, one rider leaned over to hand Pay Dirt one of the heavy bags that had been taken from the boot of the stage. Two others rode alongside and handed down the two remaining bags. Quickly, efficiently Pay Dirt stowed them under the tarp that covered the packs slung across the burro's back.

When he had finished, there was no bulge showing to give away the presence of what bags he had put there.

Joe's heart nearly stopped its beating. The screen of branches that hid him from the outlaws seemed pitifully inadequate. He remembered the prayers his mother had taught him, and he said them now, rushing through them as though by their very number he could assure himself of safety. A cold sweat beaded his forehead, although even now he could feel the chill of the crisp air gnawing through his clothes.

The next instant the five riders had rammed home their spurs and were away, while behind them hung a fog of slow-settling dust. Joe noticed that they took care to avoid the tracks Pay Dirt had made, and that they veered off to the southwest of the trail as they left.

Pay Dirt tightened one of the ropes on his pack, slapped his burro across the hindquarters with his walking stick, and went down off the bridge toward the stage. He started a small circle around it, stopping halfway to allow his burro to walk in close to the charred, smoldering mass. Beyond the scene of the robbery he swung back onto the trail and fell into his plodding stride toward the north.

Joe's fascinated gaze followed Pay Dirt Warren until he seemed a small, unmoving thing on the trail. No one knew Pay Dirt's part in the robbery, so he would have no motive for hiding. He'd go back to his shack, as if nothing had happened.

Only something has happened, Joe kept thinking.

And then he knew that unless he followed the old prospector and kept a close watch, those three heavy bags might disappear forever. He waited, letting his plan take shape, watching until he saw Pay Dirt swing off the trail where it cut in toward Rattler Cañon two miles from the bridge. Pay Dirt's slab shack lay three miles up the cañon.

Rattler Cañon flanked the hogback. Its far end was steep, but it could be climbed, and once out of it and over the ridge it wasn't one hundred yards to Pay Dirt's shack. Joe, crippled as he was, made it in twenty minutes, leaving the mare behind.

Long before Pay Dirt was within hearing distance of the shack, Joe was lying beneath a low-growing piñon less than thirty yards above. He saw Pay Dirt turn into the clearing, untie the pack ropes, and unload the supplies he had brought from town. The three sacks were thrown in with the rest and lay on the ground while the old prospector silently stabled the burro in the shed behind the shack.

The darkness came down quickly; almost before Joe knew it, Pay Dirt's moving figure was blotted out in the shadows below. But he heard him moving around, heard him make a half dozen trips out of the shack to carry in the things he had left before the door.

A lamp came on in the shack and sent a pale yellow rectangle of light across the litter of chips around Pay Dirt's chopping block outside. The friendly glow of that lamp made Joe realize, suddenly, that he was cold. The excitement, coupled with the half fear of Pay Dirt's nearness, had so far completely occupied him.

He had almost decided he would climb the cañon wall and ride for home, when he heard a sharp hoof ring on the rock of the trail. It telegraphed a warning that made him forget his numbness. Simultaneously Pay Dirt's light went out. Joe heard his door open, and caught the hint of a shadow as the prospector came out and crossed to the belt of cedars that grew around the clearing. Then someone spoke.

"Howdy, you old rock-scrubber!"

That booming voice coming out of the darkness, from below on the trail, froze Joe Egan in a paralysis of fright. He knew the voice, would know it anywhere.

"Swing that iron off me, Pay Dirt. It's me. Neal."

Pay Dirt's answering grunt of recognition was almost lost to Joe. He heard the rider below coming in toward the shack, heard him dismount and join Pay Dirt in the darkness. Pay Dirt's light went up again. The door for a moment framed Clyde Neal's big broad outline.

What could Clyde Neal's business with Pay Dirt Warren be? Joe paid that scant attention. He wanted nothing so much as to leave this place, to get away from the man whose bullet had maimed him. For in Joe Egan had grown up an almost frenzied fear of Clyde Neal. Even before the time Neal's bullet had lodged in his spine, the big Wagon Hammer boss had inspired that feeling in him. Joe had many times since his injury imagined the power in Neal's huge shoulders and hands.

Joe had come to his feet, had climbed upwards and backwards two steps, bracing himself with his crutch, when the cabin door opened again. Neal's voice came to him distinctly, and, as he looked below, he saw the man standing in the door with a heavy sack in each hand—the sacks from the stagecoach.

"The boys got away and swung over across the hills to Rim-rock," Neal was saying. "Hell, Pay Dirt, you don't have nothin' to worry about."

"But what about that kid?" came the invisible Pay Dirt's voice. "I tell you, young Egan passed me on the trail not twenty minutes before it happened. Where did he go?"

"We'll see, we'll see," came Neal's answer, intended to be soothing. "Grab that other sack and help me load it onto my saddle. I've got to ride for the spread. The posse may show up there and I don't want to be away."

It was Clyde Neal, then, who was behind the robbery. The cunning of it was brought home even to Joe Egan as he stood there, afraid to move, fearful that the Wagon Hammer boss would look up and through some magic sight see him. Clyde Neal would never be suspected as the man behind the gang that had headed across the hills to Rimrock. There was no witness, no one to give Neal away.

Pay Dirt shuffled into view the next minute, cutting in on Joe's thoughts. Joe saw the old prospector come out into the yard, saw him approach Neal, who was standing beside his ground-haltered horse.

By the dim light Joe could not follow exactly what happened. Suddenly the utter quiet of the night was broken by the explosion of a .45. The orange flame lance stabbed out from Neal's hand at Pay Dirt. The black form that was Pay Dirt's slowly settled to the ground; there was a pulpy cough, then silence.

Terror struck at Joe's heart. For the third time that day he had seen a man killed in cold blood. Clyde Neal was the killer this time. All at once the most important thing in the world to Joe Egan was to leave the spot immediately. He gave no thought now to his own safety but started the frantic climb back up the rocky face to where he had left the sorrel mare. He had taken only three quick, broken steps when he loosed a stone that went sliding downwards, rumbling dully.

Below, Clyde Neal looked up quickly. In an instant he had leaped across Pay Dirt's prostrate body. He ran into the cedars and headed for the place the noise had come from. He moved stealthily, with lightning speed, and he caught Joe Egan just short of the rim.

Joe heard him coming and his scream cut out across the night. The next instant Neal was on him. His gun slashed down at the side of Joe's head and the boy went down. Then, without a moment's hesitation, shooting from the hip, Neal thumbed the hammer of his weapon once. He did not have to look to make sure. He saw the dark welter of blood on Joe's forehead where the bullet had done its work. He turned and went down through the rocks and directly into the cabin.

It took him ten minutes to obliterate all signs with Pay Dirt's well-worn broom. He worked over to the cedars, up through them until at last he came to bare rock. Joe Egan lay above him on the rocks and Neal knew that he had left nothing up there that could give him away. In two minutes he had thrown a lighted match into the puddle of kerosene on the cabin floor and was out the door. Before the flames from the burning cabin had lighted the little clearing, Clyde Neal was a mile down the cañon.

Joe winced at the dull, throbbing pain in his head and tried not to open his eyes. But the light came to him redly through his closed lids and he opened them to see what it was that made it. He looked up into Doc Gentry's face.

For a moment he felt utterly at peace. So long as he did not move, the pulsing pain of his head was not unbearable. He wondered why Doc Gentry should be here, holding his head in his lap. He looked to the side, saw the lantern and the man holding it, George Tade. As he moved, he felt the warm stickiness along his scalp. Suddenly the raw cold bit into him, and then he remembered.

It was three minutes before they quieted him enough so that he could talk coherently. Once started, he could not stop; he poured forth the story of what he had seen that day, feeling that to tell it, all of it, was the only way that he could put the frightfulness of it out of his mind.

When he had finished, Doc Gentry looked up at George Tade and said: "George, you take Joe on home. I'm taking myself a ride."

Joe was sitting up, feeling better. The slug from Clyde Neal's gun had merely creased his forehead. In an instant he had read into Gentry's words the thing the man intended to do. He stood and found that he could move, that he was strong as ever. The pain in his head bothered him, yet Gentry had bandaged it and it would do.

"You can't go alone," he said, trying to steady his voice. "I'm riding with you."

"You're going home with George, Joe."

If George Tade had not spoken then, Joe would never have taken that long ride that night. But George did, and what he said was: "Joe's right. You're not goin' to meet Neal alone, Gentry."

Argument was futile. Gentry pleaded, then cursed them, until George finally put in: "Likely as not we'll run into the posse on the way. They'll throw in with us."

Gentry gave in then, thinking, as Joe afterwards learned, that they would certainly meet someone along the road. The news of the stagecoach robbery and the killing had spread like wildfire, and Gentry had every reason to believe that they would meet others.

But they didn't. The three-mile ride out to the Rimrock road was made in silence. Gentry had already brought Joe's mare down to the smoldering ruin of Pay Dirt's cabin, and they took the trail down Rattler Cañon to gain the road. From there it was north, away from the scene of the stage robbery; it was late and not surprising that they encountered no one.

Where the trail met the road, George Tade tried to persuade Doc to give up his revenge. But Gentry wouldn't listen. He had gone a little off balance in his hatred for Clyde Neal. All he would say was: "One of my slugs is tagged for Neal. He's got it coming and I can beat him. You two head back to town. I'll make out."

Tade couldn't agree to that, so they rode on—north over the seven long miles that took them to the Wagon Hammer. Gentry was silent for the most part, speaking only once, and then of the fact that Neal had shot Joe after hitting him over the head. Joe had been lucky—damned lucky.

When they were within sight of the Wagon Hammer, close because of the darkness, Gentry reined in and let George Tade ride alongside him.

"I know where to find Neal if he's here," he said, pointing beyond the wagon shed toward the weathered frame house ahead. "He'll be in his room at this end of the house. You and Joe ride with me as far as the well house and wait there. Cover me. If Neal gets me, you get him. Now ride quiet."

That was all, yet Joe saw that it was a perfect plan. The Wagon Hammer bunkhouse was out behind, and there was little likelihood that their approach would arouse anyone before Gentry was at the house. The well house was that dark shadow that showed against the lighter rectangle of the main building.

Gentry dismounted a little short of the wagon shed. So did George Tade and Joe Egan. Gentry and Tade had to wait a few seconds for Joe—for him to get his crutch and his .22. Joe never did learn where Gentry had found his rifle, but he supposed it was somewhere along the line of the mad dash he had made up the hill that night. At any rate, he had it now, and the feel of it made him a little more certain of his movements.

They walked slowly side-by-side as far as the well house, and there Gentry left them. The pale light of the stars was enough to make things clear from there on. It allowed them to follow Gentry's progress, to watch as he removed his right glove and pushed his coat away from the holstered six-gun at his thigh. Halfway across the bare yard, Gentry suddenly halted at the snarl of a dog that came running from out of the deeper shadow of the long porch fronting the house. Gentry made no move from there. It wasn't necessary.

As the dog snarled, a voice spoke out: "Quiet, Nip!"

By those two low-spoken words Clyde Neal announced his presence. Had they searched out the shadows, they could have seen him before. For now Joe saw that Neal leaned indolently against a porch post. The next instant he had pushed himself erect and stepped out of the shadow toward Doc Gentry. And as Neal moved, Joe moved. He went down on one knee, close in by the wall of the well house, and lined his rifle on Clyde Neal.

Beside him he heard the faint *swish* of George Tade's coat as Tade's hand brushed it aside, and Joe knew that George had drawn a gun. Neal could not have seen, for he came on until he stood within fifteen feet of Doc Gentry. The front sight of Joe's rifle was blurred, yet he carefully centered it on the pale blotch that was Clyde Neal's face and waited.

Neal drawled: "How come the visit, Doc?"

"Suppose you guess, Neal." Gentry's tones were flat. He was a man without nerves.

"I'm not answerin' riddles tonight. What do you want here?"

"Joe Egan's still alive, Neal."

Those words satisfied Clyde Neal. They heard plainly his long sigh, saw him settle back on his heels, and knew then that the time was near at hand.

The seconds passed, but neither Gentry nor Neal moved. At length Neal shifted a little, said gruffly: "I'm waitin', Gentry."

"So am I."

The suspense was maddening to Joe. His front sight dropped out of the notch of the rear one and he steadied his gun frantically. He had no faith in Gentry's beating Neal now. Neal had been raised with a six-gun in his hand and once Joe had seen the magic of that man's shooting. Thinking of this, he sensed the exact instant Neal moved.

He squeezed the trigger, but even before he felt the quick stab of the rifle at his shoulder he heard the surprising blast of Gentry's .45. His own shot merely prolonged Gentry's. The next instant Neal's head had dropped out of his sights. Unbelieving, it came to him that Gentry had beaten Clyde Neal on the draw.

Joe caught Neal's frantic forward lunge, saw the man's final effort to lift his gun. Then Neal had gone down hard and rolled over on his back. When Joe looked away, Gentry was already halfway around the corner of the house, George Tade at his heels. There were two quick shots three seconds later from the direction of the bunkhouse.

But Joe forgot all else except Clyde Neal's lifeless form before him. It was not until Gentry and George Tade had followed the four Wagon Hammer riders around the corner of the house that Joe looked away again. Gentry's and Tade's guns covered the four Wagon Hammer cowpunchers, and Horse Collar Kearney was saying: "The others are over at Rimrock, Doc. We had no part in this. They were men hired for the job."

"You've got other things to answer for, Horse Collar," Gentry said.

One by one he made them snake their broncos out of the corral and saddle up while George Tade guarded the others. When they were ready to ride, Gentry made Horse Collar sling Neal's body across his saddle and ride with it, steadying the limp form with one hand.

It was that way they rode into town, Gentry and Tade and Joe, with their guns covering the Wagon Hammer riders. They roused Troutman and had him open the jail. They took Clyde Neal's body to the undertaker's while Troutman and two or three others rode back to the Wagon Hammer to try and find the $10,000 Neal's men had taken from the boot of the stage. Joe learned then that the money was a two week's mine payroll being shipped around a bridge washout on the Rimrock-Benson line.

It was by the light of the undertaker's lamp that Doc Gentry first saw the small blue hole that centered Clyde Neal's forehead. He ripped away Neal's shirt, saw that his own bullet had gone to the right, through Neal's side. That wound would not have killed the man, would not have stopped that quick upswing of Neal's death-dealing arm.

He did not tell Joe what he had found. But that night in the clean warm kitchen of Sarah Egan's modest home, he told her about it.

"I carry a Forty-Five. So does George Tade. That was a hole made by a Twenty-Two."

"Joe shot him, then," Sarah said.

"I reckon. But why?"

"Because, next to me, I think he loves you most, Harry."

Doc flushed. "Nonsense. Why should he?"

"Why shouldn't he? Why shouldn't I . . . after all you've done for Joe?"

Doc came out of his chair like a man in a trance. But Sarah faced him, a little proud, a little humble, unashamed.

"But I thought. . . ."

"I know," Sarah said. "You've loved me, Harry. I've loved you, too, but I was married, and I stick by a bargain. You thought I didn't love you. I do. Am I shameless, Harry?"

Doc never knew whether he answered her or not. How can a man remember what he says when he holds a woman like that in his arms?

★ ★ ★ ★ ★

A Notch for Bill Dagley

★ ★ ★ ★ ★

This story was completed right after "Doc Gentry" and submitted to Popular Publications on December 21, 1936. David Manners, who edited *10 Story Western,* had suggestions for changes he wanted made. These were made by the author and the story was resubmitted on February 27, 1937. It was purchased on March 18, 1937 and Jon Glidden was paid $112.50. The title was changed to "The Cowman They Couldn't Kill" when it appeared in *10 Story Western* (8/37). For its appearance here the author's title has been restored.

I

There were some who said: "I told you so." But none of them said it to Bill Dagley's face. After what happened, they let him strictly alone. They had warned him—warned him even before he had recorded the deed that made him sole owner of the Mule Ear—that he stood a good chance of being wiped out between the two big outfits. His answer had been that any man who let the threat of a range war stand between him and the best small ranch on the Gila Bench should have his guts examined.

That answer was characteristic of Bill Dagley. He went into the thing with eyes wide open, fully realizing the troubles that were willed to him with the outfit. It surprised a few, but not many, when he decided to stick. Most of them remembered that old George Dagley, the uncle who had left the spread to Bill as his only surviving relative, had been just as stubborn. And after all, Bill Dagley was a stranger, and it was none of their business. But between themselves they gave him six months to see the wisdom of their words.

Dagley hired two riders and went to work on his spread. It wasn't long before word got around that Wes Masters, on one side of Dagley, was bringing in gun hands to swell his already sizeable Doubletree crew. And at about the same time, on the other side of Dagley, Max Harrow built an addition to his bunkhouse. That became the basis for the rumor that strange riders had been seen drifting in toward Harrow's Lazy Rattler layout on moonlight nights.

It wasn't out in the open yet, but all the elements were here for the final showdown between Masters and Harrow. And all through this, everyone wondered why it was that Bill Dagley would sit between the two and run the chance he did.

In town, one Saturday night, one of Masters's new hardcases, Sash Mayhew, emptied his six-gun pointblank at a gambler in a brawl over a percentage girl. Because a silver dollar would have covered the place where his five slugs entered the gambler's chest, people remembered Mayhew's name. It soon became apparent that he was the unnamed leader of this pack of curly wolves who were now riding for the Doubletree.

Some said that Wes Masters had gone too far in hiring men like Mayhew. Others excused him and said that the hiring was the work of Finlay Slade, Masters's foreman, who had been at the Doubletree since the accident, two years before, that crippled Wes Masters. No one doubted that Slade had done a good job of rodding the outfit, but they did say that Masters had given him a little too much authority.

The day it happened was the day the bank refused to renew Wes Masters's loan of $7,000 on his Doubletree. That surprised everyone, even though they knew that Max Harrow had had a hand in it, as director of the bank. But, somehow, they hadn't figured that Harrow would be so blunt in inviting trouble. After getting the news, Masters drove out of Broken Nose with his daughter Edith beside him on the seat of the buckboard. The two of them were sitting, straight and tight-lipped, Masters showing by the look in his eyes that things wouldn't be long in breaking.

That same day Bill Dagley was in Broken Nose completing the purchase of a long list of supplies he would be packing back to his layout late that afternoon. There lacked two weeks of the six months they had given him.

Dagley was at Overstreet's hardware store when Wart Peyson streaked into town, riding a lathered bay mare. Someone told Wart where to find his boss, and the undersized, bowlegged man clumped into Overstreet's and up to Dagley to blurt out: "Hell's busted loose, Bill!"

Len Overstreet, telling the others about it later, said that Dagley took five long seconds before he looked up from the column of figures he was adding on his bill, and then only after writing down the total. Overstreet said it was certain Dagley knew at the time what was coming, for he made a mistake of 13¢ in his addition. When Bill Dagley added figures wrong, he was plenty riled.

Dagley finally laid down his pencil. He turned to Wart and asked: "How come?"

"They cut down on Brad and fired the place," Wart told him. "Barn, wagon shed, house . . . the whole damned shootin' match! There ain't a stick left you could whittle on, Bill!"

Dagley was a big man, but he looked bigger than ever—Overstreet said—as he straightened up and looked down at Wart, asking levelly: "Where were you and Brad?"

"Ridin' the brakes like you told us," Wart explained. "Cuttin' for strays. Brad was closest and seen the smoke first. He cut loose with his iron a couple times to let me know. I saw him fog it for the layout. I was maybe a quarter mile behind, all the way in. They blew him apart as he rode up to the corral. Then they lit out and rode over the ridge . . . three of 'em. Hell, I couldn't do a thing."

Overstreet, standing behind his counter and watching, swore later that Dagley's pale blue eyes changed to a dull slate gray as he asked, quiet-like: "Who did it, Wart?"

Wart took the time to wipe his perspiring face with his bandanna before he replied, looking Dagley squarely in the eyes: "I wasn't any too close, Bill. Got a good look at only one.

He's one of the only two on this range who'd do a thing like that. You guess."

"Finlay Slade?"

Wart shook his head. "I reckon it could've been, but it wasn't."

Bill Dagley didn't move so much as a muscle. He stood there for several moments, looking like he'd known for a long time that this was coming. Finally he turned to Overstreet.

"Len," he drawled, "you hang onto this stuff I bought here a few days for me. Give me a box of Forty-Fives and a handful of Remington Thirty-Thirties."

Overstreet reached back and got the shells. Dagley laid two silver dollars on the counter, but Overstreet pushed them back, saying: "This is on the house, Bill. If you let Sash Mayhew live beyond sundown, I reckon I'll ride out myself and have a try at him."

Dagley looked down at Overstreet with a mild surprise showing behind the anger in his eyes, as though in wonder that anyone but himself could have guessed it was Sash Mayhew.

At the time, Overstreet meant what he said. But in reality, neither he nor anyone else in Broken Nose would have acted so rashly. Ever since signing on with the Doubletree, Sash Mayhew's passport had been his matched pair of Colt .44s, and no man on the range would have dared to meet him with guns if it could have been avoided. Knowing what Bill Dagley intended, Overstreet's estimation of the man went up a couple notches, although he and everyone else already liked and respected this comparative stranger.

Bill turned to Wart Peyson then. "Come over to the bank and I'll pay you off, Wart."

Wart accepted the offer with a shrug of his narrow shoulders and answered half apologetically: "You're buyin' into somethin' out o' my line, Bill."

Len Overstreet didn't blame Wart for going across with Bill

and drawing his time. Everyone agreed that Wart did the right thing to cut loose from what he knew was coming right then. He had worked for Dagley only six months. Riding was only a job, and he was no more attached to Dagley than to anyone else. The Mule Ear owner was too new in this country to have inspired any loyalties. Dagley could do one of two things—clear out until the trouble blew over, or stay and fight—and neither one was any of Wart's business.

What Bill Dagley did was surprising to some, but not to Overstreet. He had seen the look in Dagley's eyes back there in the store when Wart had brought him the news. Bill walked down the street to the jail and found Sheriff Ben Walker in his office.

"Sheriff," he told Walker, "I've got a job to do you won't like. I'm ridin' out to the Doubletree after Sash Mayhew."

Ben Walker had been among the first on this range. He had seen the rise of the Doubletree and the Lazy Rattler, and he had been a lawman, and a good one, for longer than he cared to remember. He knew why it was that Wes Masters had made a gun boss of Finlay Slade. What Bill Dagley told him certainly should have surprised any man, and undoubtedly would, but Walker's expression contained nothing but polite interest.

"I reckon you got a good reason, Bill," he answered. "Good luck."

That was all. Dagley turned and left. He headed down to the livery stable.

Sheriff Walker, like everyone else who had heard of Dagley's being burned out, thought that here was another good man throwing away his life against the Doubletree guns. The lawman had tried long ago to stop what he knew was coming. He had failed, and was now using good judgment in keeping strictly out of it.

At the livery stable, Max Harrow, who had stayed in town after the meeting at the bank, came up to Dagley as he was saddling his buckskin.

"Say the word, and I'll round up the outfit and ride out with you, Bill," he said.

But Dagley merely shook his head and answered: "Your time comes later, Harrow. Right now this is a one-man job."

Things might have turned out differently if Harrow and his Lazy Rattler crew had gone with Dagley. At the time, many doubted the sincerity of Harrow's offer, since his game up until now had been always to let Wes Masters make the first move. But he had made the offer, and everyone knew where he stood in this. He joined the rest in watching Dagley ride down the street and out of town.

Dagley didn't hurry. He knew he had plenty of time before the sun went down. It was like him to go at it this way, with a confidence no one else felt, and without too many words to condemn him if he should fail.

Six miles across the low grassy hills of the Lazy Rattler brought him within sight of his own layout—or what had been his layout—lying now, a cluster of four charred smears in a patch of brown, at the foot of a low limestone ridge that cut north through his biggest pasture.

He didn't bother to swing off the trail and ride over to look at the ruins. That could come later—after he had finished with this other matter.

He looked to the north once, toward that narrow cleft in the high, forbidding hills that ran steeply up into the snow-capped peaks of the mountains. Dagley's Notch, they called it. That narrow opening, the only pass onto the lush-grass summer range back in the hills, was the thing that had involved him in this.

Years back, Max Harrow had rodded for Wes Masters. That was before the time his father died and left him with enough money to quit Masters and buy his own outfit. Even though Masters had prior claim to the free range in the hills, Harrow had the nerve to assert his rights and use that range along with the Doubletree.

At first there was no friction, but under Harrow the Lazy Rattler herds grew until now there wasn't room for both outfits up there in the hills. They both needed it; it was too small—and the war that had threatened for years was about to break.

"And I'm in the middle," Dagley mused, half aloud. What he said was true. The only way through the Notch and onto summer range lay across the Mule Ear.

This significant fact, plus Dagley's insistence on his rights, was the thing that had involved him in whatever was to come.

II

The sun was half an hour above the horizon at his back as Dagley rode past the Doubletree cook shanty and on up to the near wing of the sprawling adobe house. Several riders who idled in front of the bunkhouse eyed him with a more than casual interest, but he paid them little notice. As he swung out of the saddle, a little stiff from the chill and the two-hour tension, he saw Wes Masters come to the door of his office, the end room of the wing.

Masters was a big man, nearly as tall as Dagley, broader, and thirty pounds heavier. It wasn't until he reached back inside the door and brought out his crutch to swing single-footed out onto the porch that one noticed his crippled leg. Two years ago the cinch of Wes Masters's saddle had snapped while he was roping. His stallion had thrown him and trampled him.

As Dagley approached across the sandy yard and met Masters's frowning stare, a look of definite hostility flashed between the two. It was Dagley who spoke first, ignoring the lack of a greeting.

"You did a good job, Masters."

The rancher's frown deepened as he queried bluntly: "What job?"

"I'd think you'd have the guts to back Finlay Slade's play."

A little color left Masters's rugged, tanned face. Men didn't often use this tone with him. "That'll bear some explainin', Dagley," he said thinly.

"Slade sent Sash Mayhew and two others over and burned me out this afternoon. They cut down on Brad Marks."

"That's a damned lie!" Masters flared, but Bill saw the doubt come into his eyes.

He ignored the rebuff, certain in reading Masters's expression that the rancher was ignorant of what had happened. It was just as he had expected to find it. Thinking this, he said: "A while ago, I told you that you were heading into trouble, letting Finlay Slade manage things for you. He's hired men like Mayhew, and now they're. . . ."

All at once he saw the girl standing in the doorway, and he checked his words. Edith Masters had evidently been with her father in the office as he rode up, and had most certainly heard their conversation. She caught Dagley's look, and stepped to her father's side.

"Father knows nothing about this," she protested.

Dagley had seen her only three times since coming to this country. He remembered each time well. The first striking impression she made on him had lasted, and now, as she stood there, straight and tall in a light blue blouse and full brown skirt, she was somehow boyish without losing the femininity that was hers through a striking beauty. Yes, he admitted that she was infinitely desirable—that the smooth, tanned face with its straight features and deep-set brown eyes held a strength of character even more pronounced than her father's—but at the same time he knew that she was a part of the thing that was destroying him.

He spoke to Masters again. "A month ago, you sent Slade over to see me. He was to arrange your drive across my place and up to summer pasture through the Notch. Did he tell you my proposition?"

"He did," Masters answered. "I sent you my answer."

Dagley nodded. "I wanted to be sure. Slade said you'd drive through anyway."

"For twelve years I drove across the Mule Ear without stirrin' up trouble with George Dagley," Masters said a little grimly. "Now you come along and lay down a set of rules no man can play to."

"You're wrong about my rules, Masters. I asked you a cut of one steer for every fifty you drove across my place. I told Slade why I was asking it. Every year George Dagley lost a full crop of alfalfa because of your driving in and out of that pasture. Last summer the loss of that crop came near to ruining him in the drought. I aim to see that the same thing doesn't happen to me. I'm entitled to that crop, and I'll be paid for it if I lose it."

Masters gave no immediate answer. Finally he asked bluntly: "Where's all this talk gettin' us, Dagley?"

"It's getting us this far," Dagley answered, aware that Edith Masters had not taken her eyes from him. "When I made the same proposition to Max Harrow, he agreed to my terms. When the Lazy Rattler pushes through the Notch, I'm to be paid for it."

"Max Harrow and I don't run things the same way. You know what I think of him. This mornin' his bank turned down my loan . . . when I've got all this to back it up." He waved a hand to indicate the broad sweep of rolling range, dotted with grazing herds.

Dagley paused. Further words seemed futile, but because of the girl he felt the need to give his reasons for what he was going to do. He told them: "All this is proof that your outfit fired my place."

"What proof is that?" Masters asked irritably. "Do you think I'd burn out a man, Dagley?"

"No, I don't. But I know Slade would. I know he did. Wart Peyson recognized Sash Mayhew as one of the three who cut down on Brad."

"Father didn't do this," Edith Masters put in. "Neither did Finlay Slade. Wart Peyson was wrong."

"No," Dagley said, not looking at her, speaking to Masters. "You've made a gun boss of Slade, and you're to blame for what he does."

"What I do is my own affair," Masters answered. "Slade's a good man. How far would I get if I didn't have guns to keep Max Harrow off?" He tapped the thigh of his crippled leg. "I'm sorry you were burned out, Dagley, but you can't lay the blame on this outfit. What do you aim to do?"

Down below, the *clanging* of the supper bell at the cookshanty sounded out across the still air. Dagley turned to look toward the bunkhouse, seeing the riders going in through the door for their evening meal.

He faced Masters again. "I'm going down there after Sash Mayhew. Maybe Finlay Slade, too."

Edith Masters's eyes widened in alarm. She put her hand on her father's arm, breathing: "Don't let him do it."

"Sash'll kill you, Dagley," Masters echoed her thoughts. "Stay away from him until I get this settled."

"After I'm through with this, I'm riding for the Lazy Rattler," Dagley went on as though they hadn't spoken. "From now on I'm Max Harrow's man."

Here it was, bluntly put, but the only way Dagley saw to do it. The sun-wrinkled face of Wes Masters was a study. A smoldering rage took the warmth out of his blue eyes, and his lips compressed into a hard line. Masters carried no weapon or he would have used it now, Dagley knew. To see the man's massive figure leaning so helplessly on his crutch showed clearly what a torture it was to him to be without the use of his legs.

"So that's the way it is?"

Dagley nodded.

"Then tell Harrow it's war, Dagley . . . that is, if you live to tell him. I've been waitin' too long for this."

There was nothing more to say. Dagley studied the girl's face. She was pale, but the tilt to her chin made it clear enough that she stood with her father.

He turned and left them. It was only a short distance to the bunkhouse, yet he went into the saddle and rode down, close in to the door.

They must have seen him coming, for when he stepped in through the narrow door every man at the table was facing him. The table ran crosswise at the end of the single large room, to the left of the door. Dagley's glance shuttled once to the far end, and saw that the bunks were empty.

Finlay Slade sat at the head of the table, Sash Mayhew beside him, with his back to the wall. Dagley's attention centered on the two. A stillness had greeted his entrance, and now it held so that his words, spoken in a low voice, carried clearly: "I want to see you, Sash."

To men such as these, Dagley's words held a thinly veiled threat. As if standing apart and witnessing the scene, Dagley understood then what a trust Wes Masters had placed in Finlay Slade in letting him pick this crew. They were an odd assortment, hard and shifty-eyed and all wearing their guns tied low. Sash Mayhew had been Slade's first find. The rest were like him, although he was admittedly the best among them.

It was Slade they looked to now, and it was he who reached over to put a hand on Sash Mayhew's arm. He pulled the little gunman back into his chair as he himself rose to his feet: "What the hell do you mean by busting in here like this, Dagley?" he growled. He stood there, a dominating figure, tall and wide of shoulder and handsome in a rough way. Finlay Slade looked all man.

"You can buy into this after I'm through with Sash," Dagley answered. "Get onto your feet, Mayhew! Wart Peyson saw you today."

Sash Mayhew's thin, unshaven face took on a mirthless smile. He got up slowly, Slade making no attempt to stop him now. "Wart never could see good, Dagley," he drawled.

The words were unnecessary. Sash uttered them merely to play for those precious seconds that would allow him to set the stage for what he knew was coming. Once on his feet, his spare frame made the twin Colts at his thighs look bigger than they really were. His hands, long and with tapering fingers, looked almost delicate.

Slade muttered something to Mayhew, and stepped back and out of the way. Between these three lay a common understanding. Dagley knew too much. He had come looking for trouble, and Slade and Sash were playing for the excuse to wipe him out. Those at Slade's end of the table sensed what was coming and followed their leader's example, pushing back out of the way.

Slade started to speak: "What did Wart Peyson have to . . . ?"

Suddenly Sash Mayhew's downhanging arm moved surely and swiftly. No man there had ever seen Bill Dagley use a six-gun—otherwise, they would have known what was coming. Now to see the smooth flash of his hand that planted his Colt at his hip brought a distinct shock. Dagley even had that extra split second to make sure of his aim, so fast was his draw against the man who lived by his guns. His .45 exploded the dead quiet and marked the exact instant Sash's thin frame jerked convulsively.

No man could have stood up under the terrific impact of that slug. Viciously Dagley had thrown his bullet angling at the table top, so that the lead hit the slab and flattened before it took Mayhew low in the stomach. It knocked the little gunman backward into the wall. With a scream of agony he forgot his weapon and dropped it, hands clawing at the red smear below his belt.

The others were quick, but not quick enough. Dagley's .45 swung to cover them and freeze them in their half-crouching attitudes. Hands came away from gun butts as Dagley took a backward step that put him alongside the door. Mayhew toppled face down onto the floor and lay there with a stunned, helpless look. Dagley didn't leave then. He waited a moment longer, relishing the bewildered fright that settled over Finlay Slade's face.

"Some other time, Slade . . . when we're alone," came Dagley's quiet words.

Then he stepped out through the door. They heard the *creak* of saddle leather before the quick pound of hoofs brought them out of their surprise. Slade bellowed a hoarse oath and lunged for the door. As he showed in it, the hollow snort of a .45 blasted once outside, and he sprawled back inside the room again. A bullet had splintered the frame within two inches of his head.

III

Later, as a waning moon dropped toward the distant jagged horizon to give him light, Bill Dagley rode down off the ridge and toward the still smoldering piles of ruins that had been his Mule Ear buildings but a short twelve hours before. From the top of the ridge he had five minutes ago seen three moving shadows down by his corral. He was riding down there now to discover who it was that took such an interest in the Mule Ear in his absence.

He came on warily, reining in while the distance was still too great for accurate shooting, challenging: "Who's there?"

"That you, Dagley?" came a voice. "It's me . . . Harrow."

Here was something unexpected. He had planned on riding to the Lazy Rattler later that night to see Harrow. Finding him here now might save him a trip. He rode on, recognizing the other two as Link Jamison and Bob Temple, two Lazy Rattler riders. Harrow's thick-set figure was the shortest of the three.

"We rode over to bury Brad," Max Harrow told him as he dismounted.

"Much obliged," Dagley answered, seeing that Jamison leaned on a shovel near a mound of newly turned earth. He was glad to be saved this task.

"Sash wasn't there?" Harrow queried.

"Sash is dead."

Link Jamison straightened from his slouch, and Bob Temple's gasp was clearly audible. Harrow stood, silent and unmoving, for a long moment, somehow betraying in his very stolidity the shock Dagley's words had carried.

"You leavin' the country, Bill?" he finally asked.

It had never occurred to Bill Dagley to ride away from trouble. Now, finding that these men and the rest had thought of his doing such a thing sent a flood of unreasoning anger through him. "There's nothing I know of to run from."

Max Harrow's low laugh seemed strangely out of place, but the next instant his words gave it meaning. "I could use you, Bill. What do you aim to do?"

Dagley realized then that nothing would carry more weight with Max Harrow than a man's ability to use his guns. He watched as the rancher flicked a match and held it to the stub of his cigarette. In the orange radiance of the flame his heavy features were thrown into garish planes of light and shadow, heightening a blunt ugliness that Dagley knew was a mirror of his nature. Harrow had an untiring energy, a limitless ambition, and a fearlessness that were not to be denied.

He knew the man just well enough to realize that he wouldn't have chosen his side under any other circumstances. Yet he had no choice here, and his mind was made up. Regardless of that, he would make his own terms and, thinking this, he framed his answer: "I reckon I'll play a lone hand. Slade's the man I'm after."

Harrow was a long time answering. He snapped out the match, held it poised in his fingers a moment, and then flipped it to the ground. "You won't get far by yourself, Bill. Throw in with me. Then you can tell Wes Masters and Ben Walker to go to hell."

"Ben Walker?"

Harrow nodded. "Don't you figure they'll send the law after you for cuttin' down on Sash? That is . . . unless you come in with me? Walker knows enough not to stick his foot into my business."

"Then you're making my business yours?"

"I am," Harrow stated. "The Doubletree burned you out. That throws you on my side whether you like it or not."

There was no denying this argument. Harrow's manner was blunt, as always, but Dagley took no offense.

"Wes Masters asked me to tell you he's for war from now on," he told Harrow. "If siding with you will get me a chance at Finlay Slade, I'm with you."

"Finlay Slade carries out Wes Masters's orders, Dagley. We're buckin' Masters."

"Either way you put it adds up to the same with me."

That seemed to satisfy Harrow. He stood a moment longer, looking at Dagley, and then turned to Link Jamison and Bob

Temple. "We'll be ridin'," he said. "We have an hour to get to Sundog Creek."

If Bill Dagley was at first surprised to hear Harrow mention the dry wash that cut through Wes Masters's north pasture, the next four hours doubled his surprise. In that time he learned that plans had been laid for striking at the Doubletree long before he himself had been burned out. Those four hours took them onto Doubletree range where three more of Harrow's crew joined them to help push two hundred head of Wes Masters's steers deep into the badlands to the east.

It took them most of the night to do a thorough job of it—to satisfy Harrow until he finally told them: "Let's head for home, boys. If they can gather up this herd in less'n two weeks, they're better in the saddle than they are with guns . . . which is sayin' a lot."

Dawn caught them within five miles of the Lazy Rattler, safely off Doubletree range. Later, coming abruptly within sight of the outfit's unpainted frame buildings, the welcome sight of smoke from the cook shanty chimney whetted their gnawing hunger. They unsaddled quickly and went in to their breakfast. Bill Dagley devoured his food in silence, sensing in the others a certain respect that could come from nothing other than the news of his meeting with Sash Mayhew.

After they had finished the meal and were idling in front of the bunkhouse, smoking, Max Harrow came down from the house. He walked up to Dagley and faced the rest of them.

"Gents, this is Bill Dagley," he said. "He's one of the outfit. See that he gets a bunk, Link."

In this simple way, Harrow introduced the new member to his crew. Looking them over, Dagley saw that they had been chosen wisely. There were several men, like Jamison, Foley, and Temple, who had ridden for Harrow for years. There were new faces, too, faces that reminded Dagley of those he had seen the evening before at the Doubletree. With this mixture of men who were loyal to him and those who were being paid for the use of their guns, Harrow had welded together a real fighting outfit.

"From here on out there'll be plenty of powder burned and plenty of night riding," Harrow went on. "Any man who wants to saddle up and ride, still has the right to do it." He paused briefly. Not one in the circle about him moved. "Five of you turn in and get some sleep . . . Link, Bog, Dagley, Corbin and O'Connor. The rest of you go spell the boys in the east pasture. If trouble's comin', it'll come from that way."

Sleep did not come to Bill Dagley at once. He was weary to the bone, yet there were things on his mind that would not let him close his eyes. He felt little regret in killing Sash Mayhew. The little gunman, like several others along Dagley's back trail, had picked the wrong man to go against, and had discovered too late his uncanny swiftness with a gun.

He no longer doubted Wes Masters's guilt in what had happened. The man was so warped in his hatred for Harrow that he would let nothing stand in his way of having full claim on the free pasture beyond the Notch. Even the memory of Edith Masters made little difference to Dagley now. His instinct had been to trust her, but that instinct had played him false and made him feel a little unsure of himself. The girl was like her father, sharing his ambitions, his hatreds, and knowing and approving of every move he made. He could not bring himself to hate the two of them, but he would feel no regrets over anything that might happen.

That evening, Harrow sent for Jamison, O'Connor, and Dagley. "You three are headin' up to the Doubletree line camp above the Pinnacles," he told them when they were in his office. "I want you to burn it down. Don't use your hardware unless you have to, but burn that shack and barn. Link, you better take along a couple quarts o' coal oil."

Link Jamison, tall and thin and looking a little cadaverous with his gaunt unshaven face, swallowed with difficulty. "Ain't that ridin' it a little too heavy, boss?" he drawled. He had been with the Lazy Rattler since the beginning and was a hard-working, unimaginative man who knew the seriousness of the thing Harrow proposed.

"I'm makin' this fight my own way," Harrow replied deliberately. "I've told you once you can ride out of it. No one's stoppin' you now, Link."

For a moment the light of anger was in Jamison's eyes. Then his glance fell, and he muttered, a little ashamed: "Forget I mentioned it."

Ten minutes later saw them saddled and riding out into the star-studded night. The bunkhouse was deserted when they left; the others had gone ahead of them, by twos and threes, riding on errands as ominous as their own. Max Harrow was playing his hand strongly.

Three miles to the east they went through a gate and onto Mule Ear range, leaving the hills and striking out across the bench-like two mile stretch that sloped gradually upward toward the shadow of the distant Notch. All at once Dagley's buckskin missed stride and threw a shoe off the right front. A mile farther on he went lame.

"You better ride back and catch up another bronc', Dagley," Link Jamison advised. "We'll wait for you over by your east fence. Hell, we got all night for this job."

So it was agreed that Dagley should return to the Lazy Rattler. He took his time on the way back, saving the buckskin. As the shadowy cluster of buildings finally lifted out of the gray distance, he made directly for the corral. He unsaddled the gelding and was snaking out his rope with his eye on a rangy black when he heard the slow beat of hoofs above on the trail.

It was not in Bill Dagley's nature to be curious, but when the sound faded into the night's stillness up near the house, he remembered suddenly that the Lazy Rattler was deserted. Who would be riding in here along the trail that came down through the hills from the direction of the Doubletree?

His curiosity aroused, he made his way up past the bunkhouse as quietly as he could, then over to the rear stoop of the house. No light showed along the side or back, so he went along the wall to the front. Standing there in the thick shadowless darkness at the corner of the house, he looked out and saw the wiry chestnut mare that stood hip-shot at the hitch rail close by. Even at this distance he could make out the animal's jaw brand, the shallow U-shaped tracing of the Doubletree.

There had been no hint of what he was to find. Even after he had put down his first surprise, he reasoned that there must be some logical explanation for the presence of this night rider from the enemy's camp. He could see, from here, the light in Harrow's office. Prying into another man's affairs was distasteful to him, yet it was possible that Harrow was in danger. So he edged quietly along to the window and stooped to look in through the two-inch slit under the drawn blind.

Finlay Slade sat on the scarred oak desk in the center of the tiny room, one leg hooked over the corner of it, facing Harrow who was eased back in his swivel chair with hands locked behind his head. The shock of seeing these two together hit Dagley like an icy blast of air bathing his body. Slade was speaking, and his voice carried faintly through the closed window.

". . . don't know . . . doin', Max . . . Sash flat-footed . . . draw. He's poison, I . . . rid of him . . . cave in a cutbank . . . before it's too late."

IV

A cold fury settled through Dagley as he saw Harrow gesture as though to wave aside Slade's fears. His answer came in a deeper tone than Slade's, carrying clearly: "Let me run this my way, Slade. You did one hell of a job in lettin' Wart Peyson spot Sash and ride in with the news. If it hadn't been for that, Dagley wouldn't be huntin' Masters down right now."

Slade's face reddened in anger, yet his glance fell before Harrow's direct stare and he mumbled some unintelligible reply.

Dagley had seen enough. He took two steps that put him in front of the door. Raising a booted foot, he kicked the panel open, stepping in as it swung with a *crash* against the wall.

The interruption brought Harrow halfway out of his chair, brought Slade down off the desk in a half crouch of readiness. Bill Dagley stood framed in the doorway, hands hanging loosely at his sides, waiting. Neither man facing him completed that involuntary gesture toward his six-gun. Slade straightened up, careful to hook his thumbs in his belt, while Harrow eased back into his chair, his blunt fists clenched in plain sight on the desk top.

"I thought you rode out with Link, Dagley." There was a belligerence in Harrow's tone that might have been an attempt to bolster his confidence.

Dagley ignored it, ignored the man altogether, as his glance settled on Slade. "Just a little social call?" he asked.

"Slade's here on business," Harrow put in quickly. "I want to know what you are doin' here."

Dagley held his answer for a long moment. At length he said: "I reckon what I've learned tonight will come in mighty handy. Maybe Wes Masters won't be glad to hear about this."

Behind him, Dagley heard a light footfall at the precise instant Harrow's narrow-lidded eyes showed a quick surprise. Sensing his danger, Dagley whirled, his hand flashing to the six-gun at his thigh. But when he caught the dull glitter of reflected lamplight from the blued steel of the Colt .45 Edith Masters held lined at him, he arrested his move.

She swung the weapon in a tight arc that menaced all three. "Wes Masters will know about this," she said in a low voice. "I've followed you all the way, Slade."

The tight-lipped expression on her face and a heightening of her rich olive coloring were the only signs that betrayed her tension. Dagley experienced sudden admiration for the girl that erased all his doubts about her.

"I can take care of these two for you," he said.

"No. You're in this with the rest," came her surprising answer. In emphasis, she swung her weapon over to line it at him.

"These two framed me and are framing your father," he insisted. "Let me help."

She shook her head, her chin coming up in clear defiance. "I'll shoot the first one of you that makes a move."

She looked away from Dagley, over to Slade, and in that instant Harrow lunged. The man's wiry body lifted the heavy desk and turned it over. Dagley was caught from behind, low down along the backs of his thighs, and lost his balance. Edith Masters swung her Colt back at him. He struck out with his right hand as he saw it come. It exploded not three feet from him and he felt a searing pain along his right arm above the elbow. Then he hit the floor, the desk pinning his legs.

Slade darted in from the side to pin the girl's arms while Harrow lunged around the desk and threw himself on Dagley, knees planted in the small of his back. His blunt fist chopped down to numb the hand Dagley stabbed out in an attempt to reach the weapon the girl had dropped.

Then Dagley watched helplessly while Harrow picked up the weapon and raised it. He felt the blow coming. When it crashed against his skull, white sheets of light danced before his eyes and suddenly faded into a lowering blackness.

It was the light that dazzled him. He tried to shut his eyes against the red glare that heightened the fierce throb in his head. Finally, weary of the effort, he opened his eyes and looked across the dimly lit office to make out the turned-down lamp sitting on the desk.

His hands were laced tightly to his sides and his feet bound so surely that a numbness had taken away all the feeling. His right arm felt sticky above the elbow. He was lying on it, so he rolled over. Instantly he felt the bite as the dry air hit the wound. Now he could see Edith Masters.

She was tied securely in a chair and sat looking down at him. Sight of her made Dagley forget his throbbing head, the wound in his arm. In her eyes he read a look that was different from anything he had ever seen there.

"I'm sorry, Bill Dagley," she said, her voice low and throaty. "I should have known enough to trust you."

There was no answer he could give. To see her humble herself before him made her finer in his eyes, and he found it hard to stand the emptiness that hit him when he realized how little mercy she could expect from these two men.

His searching glance ran over the gear that littered the room—two saddles, a half dozen broken bridles, and, hanging on the wall, two rifles and a shotgun. He gave up any thought of reaching these, feeling the weakness that had sapped his vitality. But at last he saw something that gave him hope—a half-inch length of a rusty nail that stuck out at the base of the desk's side panel.

He inched his way to it, rubbing his wrists raw on the rough floor, not minding the pain, now that Edith Masters had spoken.

Once against the desk, he pushed himself up and started sawing the things that bound his wrists, against the point of that nail.

They found him there five minutes later. There was a brutal sneer on Harrow's wide mouth as he stepped over to plant his huge fist on Dagley's shirt front and haul him to his feet.

"Look who's tryin' to get loose!" he jeered, turning to show Slade his prisoner's bleeding wrists. He doubled up his fist and raised it, swinging a short, choppy blow that caught Dagley fully in the mouth and knocked him across the room.

Dagley shut his eyes against the pain and felt his paralyzed legs give way under him. He realized that all the potential brutality of the man was coming to the surface, now that Harrow had no reason for keeping it in check. He opened his eyes when he heard Harrow cross the room, and saw him standing before Edith Masters.

"Lay off the girl," Slade growled from where he stood just inside the door. "You'd better be thinkin' of a way out of this."

"I know of one," Harrow replied, looking down at the girl with a mirthless smile that was full of gloating satisfaction. "Wes Masters is robbin' the bank in town tonight."

Edith's eyes widened in disbelief.

Catching her expression, Harrow laughed crazily, and went on: "Yesterday the bank refused to give Masters money. Tonight he's goin' in to take it anyway."

"Talk sense," Slade said, disgust in his tone. "Wes Masters wouldn't do a thing like that."

"We're doin' it for him," Harrow stated. He turned all at once to the desk and opened a drawer. Out of it he lifted a bunch of keys and held them up to show Slade. "Here's all we need. The key to the rear door of the bank and the one to the small safe. I learned the combination to the vault two months ago . . . read it in the case of old Hargood's watch one night where he put it in the pot in a poker game." He paused watching the effect of his words.

"We'll never get away with it," Slade drawled, yet in his eyes there was a gleam of understanding that belied his words.

"We'll spit two ways . . . even," Harrow went on, disregarding the other. "You should get twenty thousand. Is it worth that for you to head down across the border and lose yourself?"

Slade made no answer for a moment, but when he did speak, he showed plainly that the idea was taking hold. "How do we deal Wes Masters a hand in this?"

"There's two Doubletree bronc's out front," Harrow explained. "Yours and the girl's. They'll be found staked out in that dry wash that runs behind the street in town. You'll trade boots and spurs with Dagley, leave your gun lyin' on the floor. We take only banknotes and securities . . . stuff that'll burn. Dynamite can do the rest . . . half a dozen sticks of it."

"What do you mean dynamite?" Slade asked in a hushed voice, for he could already see what was coming.

Harrow's answer was a wave of the hand that indicated Dagley and Edith Masters.

An utter quiet filled the room for brief seconds, to be broken at last by Edith Masters's choked sob. Dagley, unable to trust his reason, was looking at Slade. The Doubletree foreman had gone a sickly pale, but in his eyes was a shrewd look that blasted Dagley's last hopes.

"The girl, too?" Slade asked, his voice hard-edged.

Harrow shrugged his heavy shoulders. "If you know a better way, Slade. . . ." He left the sentence unfinished.

It was then that Bill Dagley went berserk with rage. With superhuman strength he struggled to his feet. Harrow, hearing the sound, whirled and faced him. When Dagley stood upright, unable to move farther against the ropes that held him, Harrow took a single step that put an added weight behind the blow he whipped out. Glassy-eyed, Dagley made no move to avoid it.

The blow caught him on the point of the jaw, snapping his head back against the wall. He fell slowly, with the tension of the ropes taking up his suddenly yielding weight. He dropped sideways and his head struck Edith Masters's knees, to break a fall that would otherwise have killed him.

V

An insistent, brain-jarring pain brought Dagley rudely back to consciousness. He opened his eyes to look in Max Harrow's unsmiling face and to feel the man's open-handed slap hit him once more in the face. The killing lust rose up in Dagley, and he struggled weakly until the effort left him exhausted. Harrow knelt, looking at him a moment longer, and then reached back to lift a rusty tin dipper off the floor and throw the water it contained in his prisoner's face. With the shocking chill of it, Dagley's brain cleared.

His mouth was dry and he tried to close it, only to find that a gag had been stuffed between his teeth. They were in the bank. He saw that instantly, for off to one side of Harrow the three tellers' cages were silhouetted in the far shadows where the light from the unshaded, low-burning lamp on the floor failed to dispel the gloom.

He struggled again, wondering what it was that held him so helpless, only to find that he was tied to one of the upright supports that braced the counter running the half length of the room beyond the cages. His boots felt loose. He looked down and saw that they weren't his own, but the finely tooled pair Finlay Slade had been wearing.

"C'mon, Max," came Slade's voice. "Everything's ready. Let's get away from here."

Dagley turned his head to search out the voice. The scene burned itself into his brain in every clear detail: Slade was standing ten feet away, spraddle-legged in front of the yawning blackness of the open vault, his face a little pallid and a grim tautness about his thin lips. Edith Masters was standing farther down along the counter, gagged and tied to one of the counter legs. The quarter-inch strands of rope were cutting the smoothness of her dress into swelling ridges. Six sticks of dynamite, wound with rope, lay in a bundle not three feet from her. Out of one end of it projected the shiny copper cylinder of the cap with a four-foot length of black fuse trailing across the floor. One of Slade's bone-handled .45s lay on the floor near the vault door, and a carelessly piled stack of paper money was on the floor at the end of the counter.

Edith Masters turned her head and looked at Dagley. The fear he read in her mute stare only added to his torment. It would be only minutes now—minutes until that bundle of dynamite blasted the girl and himself into eternity.

The only traces left after that, beyond the smear of raw flesh and blood, would be Slade's six-gun and maybe a piece of one of his boots that Dagley now wore—or perhaps one of Edith's rings and the buckle of her dress.

Fire would do the rest. Wes Masters could shout his denials to the winds; there would be mute evidence to contradict his story—evidence that he had sent his foreman and his daughter to get the money the bank had failed to loan him. Dagley's own disappearance would be logically explained away by what had happened during the last two days.

Harrow seemed to sense his thoughts. He nodded. "Figured it out pretty well, didn't I, Dagley?" he drawled. "You and the girl will be out of the way, and Wes Masters will have a noose around his neck." Silent laughter shook his wide frame. Then he noticed something, and knelt down to pull Dagley's belt off, saying: "This might give us away."

"Why the hell are you takin' so long?" Slade growled, his voice panicky in a half whisper.

Harrow gave one more look around, and then stepped over to kneel beside the bundle of dynamite. He flicked alight a match and held it to the end of the fuse. The *hissing* sputter of the fuse as it caught sent a ribbon of smoke curling lazily upward.

They moved fast then, gathering up the money that had come out of the vault. Slade went first, Harrow lingering long enough to look back once more. Then he disappeared and the back door closed softly after him. Edith Masters and Bill Dagley were alone. . . .

That sputtering length of fuse held Bill Dagley's eyes fixed in a weird fascination. In that flashing instant when death seemed settling down, he could find no regrets. But then he thought of the girl and of the disgrace that would come to her name. He thought of Harrow, and the utter ease with which the man had overcome his own feeble efforts. A cool, calculating calmness took hold of Bill Dagley then, and he told himself: *I won't die!*

He tried to bend his knees and found that he could stand the pain as the ropes cut into his flesh. He braced himself and strained every muscle in an upward push. His weakness appalled him, yet he would not give up. Finally he felt the counter leg give a little. Then suddenly the nails let loose and he rolled sideways to the floor.

Fitfully that sputtering flame crawled along the length of the fuse, leaving behind a ribbon of gray ash. Twelve feet separated Dagley from the dynamite. He put his feet against the inside face of the counter and pushed out of its reach. Lying as he was on his face, he had no way of working himself farther, so he rolled over. As he eased onto his back, he felt the stabbing prick of two nails in the counter-leg that were driving into the flesh between his shoulders.

He rolled back and lay there a brief instant, trying to think of some other way. Finding none, he steeled himself against the pain, and turned over again. He would have cried out in agony but for the gag in his mouth. The nails drove deeply into the flesh, but the pain drove him on.

145

Inch by inch he edged out toward that bundle of death, bending his knees and drawing up his legs and pushing against the smooth floor. He could see Edith Masters, could catch the wide-eyed look of horror she had fastened at a point beyond him. But he dared not look at the fuse now.

Sweat ran down off his brow. The weakness that filtered through him was a torture he had never before experienced. He worked around beside the neat stack of white sticks and at last pushed over until it lay midway the length of his body.

A last hasty, glance showed him the fuse swinging clear of the floor, the glow of the flame climbing rapidly. It seemed an eternity before he got into position with his back to it so that his hands, which were tied behind him, could reach it. Then his hands touched the coolness of those rounded sticks and he pushed back against the searing burn of the fuse.

It blistered his hands, but he shut his fingers on the fuse and rolled away. He felt the fuse give and suddenly come loose, and he looked back to see that it had pulled out of the cap. His hands went suddenly numb, and he could not open his fingers. The fuse burned to an ash in his grasp, leaving a lingering agony that twice multiplied the scorching of the powder. The room whirled before his eyes as a faintness hit him.

How long it was before he summoned the strength to move he never knew. When at last he tried to close his fingers, he felt a growing wonder mount above the pain. His hands were free! The fuse had burned through the thongs at his wrists.

A thought flashed through his mind that same instant to put all the torturing agony of his burns aside. Harrow would wait within hearing distance for the sound of the explosion. When he failed to hear it—he would come back. Harrow had no choice, for his safety lay only in his destroying the evidence that would condemn him.

It'll be this all over again! he told himself. And with thought of it he was moving—edging his way toward the open vault, toward Finlay Slade's .45 Colt that lay there on the floor.

As he worked, he kept twisting his arms. When he had pushed himself with his head through the vault door, his right arm was free below the elbow, and he could reach out and close his stiff fingers on the handle of the gun. The cool feel of the horn butt plates was soothing against the seared flesh of his palm.

He heard the faint *creak* of the back door just as he squirmed up to a sitting position against the door to the vault. Harrow had come back!

Dagley was facing the far side of the room, his eyes searching for the first hint of movement there. He held the Colt out of sight behind his thigh.

Max Harrow's light gray Stetson became a blur in the far shadows—coming toward Dagley. Then he could see the man's face, make out his slitted, hard-eyed look. He could see Finlay Slade, farther back, and the dull glint of the weapon he held in his hand.

Harrow came into the light and stopped just inside the opening at the end of the counter. Slade edged past him and raised his weapon, only to have it knocked down again as Harrow stabbed out his fist.

"Don't be a damn' fool," Harrow breathed in a hoarse whisper. "Drag him over there and lace him up again. I'll fix another fuse."

Dagley let Slade get within six feet of him before he lifted the .45. He caught the astonished look that crossed Slade's darkly handsome face, and saw the man swing up his own weapon. Then Dagley's thumb slipped off the hammer, and his Colt bucked into a blasting roar.

The slug took Slade fully in the chest, knocked him backwards, and his six-gun *clattered* hollowly to the board floor an instant before he toppled onto it.

Harrow moved before Dagley's stiff thumb could again fight back the stubborn hammer weight of his gun. Harrow was fast. His weapon blurred up into position and lanced flame in a deafening roar. Dagley felt the bone-crushing slam of the bullet against his left shoulder. Braced against the wall, his body only quivered.

His own .45 slammed against his palm a brief instant later. Harrow spun sideways with his right hip bone shattered, and the second shot he whipped out went wide of its mark. He fell to one knee, swinging his weapon back again, a brutal sneer curling down his lower lip. Dagley's .45 blasted the echoes again—and again.

Twice, Harrow's frantic effort to line his six-gun was met by a terrific slug blow that pushed him off balance. His left arm hung uselessly, shattered at the elbow. His Levi's at his thigh were a smear of blood.

Dagley saved that last bullet, coolly taking his aim and waiting until Harrow had once more turned to face him. Harrow was flicking his Colt into line with a last desperate effort. Then Dagley squeezed the trigger and the buck of the gun tore it loose from his weak grasp. Before his eyes, Harrow's flat nose became a bloody shapeless pulp. The man's head dropped limply onto his chest and he settled back onto his heels, to sit there, unmoving.

Seconds later, Ben Walker thought he was looking in at three dead men. For that reason, the first thing he did was to kneel beside the girl and take the gag from her mouth and untie her. When she was free, she pushed by the lawman and crawled over to Bill Dagley and pillowed his head against her breast, sobbing quietly.

Walker leaned down to take Dagley's bleeding wrist between his fingers. What he felt there made him straighten and look beyond the counter to inspect the faces of the crowd that had gathered before the teller's cage.

"Doc!" he bellowed. "Get in here! Quick!"

Old Doc Olsen shuffled in and laid his black bag on the floor. He grumbled something to the girl, but she didn't hear him. She bent her head to kiss Bill Dagley's pale cheek.

Two minutes later, Olsen straightened up and told the sheriff gruffly: "He'll live. But I could do better with a little more room to work in."

Dagley's eyes opened then, and he looked up at the physician. But only Edith Masters heard him say: "Don't send her away yet, Doc."

★ ★ ★ ★ ★

STONE WALLS

★ ★ ★ ★ ★

This story was submitted to Rogers Terrill, editor of Popular Publications' flagship Western pulp magazine, *Dime Western,* on May 27, 1937 and was purchased almost immediately, the author being paid $98.10. Jon Glidden's title was "Stone Walls Make a Town Tamer" and this title was retained when it appeared in *Dime Western* (9/37). For its appearance here the title has been abbreviated.

I

He was kneeling on hands and knees, his face in the cool of the clear-watered pool, drinking, just as the sibilant dry *rattle* filled the hot midday stillness. It sent him to his feet, his hand streaking to his thigh.

But there was no holstered gun there, and the *slap* of his open palm against his flat thigh muscle was a mockery that brought a flash of puzzlement from deep within his slate-gray eyes. And then, as memory supplied the reason for the absence of the weapon, those eyes went hard and flinty with an inner rage, and he stood there cursing, until at length the edge wore off his temper.

He picked up a rock and killed the rattler with one clean, hard blow and stood for a minute longer watching impassively the death flailing of the snake. Then he went on back to where his dun gelding stood hip-shot in the bright sun glare, and swung up into the hot saddle.

This was Lee Anders, eleven days out of Yuma, four days late on reporting for his parole. This was Lee Anders—without guns! The irony of the thing rankled him like an open sore. For he had lived by his guns for as long as he could remember, not wickedly, but according to the dictates of a strong-willed man who will fight for what is rightfully his. And because, four years ago, he had shot a crooked tinhorn in the throat, they had sent him to Yuma.

For the past eleven days he had taken his own good time,

nursing his grudge against the law that still held him. But now Sage City lay on the horizon ahead, a dark smear against the greens and browns of this rolling range; in Sage City, he would find Tom Kinnard.

More than once he had asked himself why they were paroling him to Tom Kinnard, the ex-marshal and gunfighter, now retired as a prosperous rancher. Rumor had it that Kinnard had gone soft and put his guns away and that he now worked and preached against the very men he had sided in former years.

It could be worse, Lee told himself, for the one hundredth time since leaving the prison gates. After all, Kinnard had promised a job, riding, at forty and beans.

An hour and a half later he rode into the far end of Sage City's dusty street. Low-walled adobes and false-fronted stores, hitch rails lined with broncos and buckboard teams, awninged walks and the ever-present loungers in front of the saloons—the scene was the same here as back in his own Gila Bend country. Yet he was grudgingly thankful to be seeing it, for his freedom had not lost its newness.

His craving was for a drink, for back along the trail the ominous signal of the rattler had cut short the quenching of his thirst. So he turned in toward the tie rail that flanked the Catamount Saloon. He was eight feet short of the swing doors when two muffled blasts cut loose from inside the saloon. An instant later the batwing doors burst outward and through the opening staggered a man with a pair of .45s in his blunt fists. Lee recognized him instantly. This was Baldy Mason, two years out of Yuma, and with the well-earned reputation of a killer in the dimness of his back trail. Baldy was roaring drunk now, that was plain enough.

The walks to either side of Baldy cleared instantly as the loungers there scattered into the shelter of neighboring doorways. He looked about him, his broken-nosed face set in a scowl. All at once he spied Lee in a liquor-dulled glance that held no sign of recognition, and he grinned mirthlessly at having found a target. Abruptly he swiveled the six-shooter in his right hand and thumbed back the hammer three times in deafening gun thunder.

The second slug whipped past Lee's face so closely that he felt its air rush. On the heel of it, he was rolling out of his saddle on the offside of the gelding. He lit on all fours in the dust as the animal reared and broke away at a run.

"Lay off, Baldy!" he shouted, crouching, unprotected, a dozen feet out from the walk. But Baldy's only answer was another whipped-out shot that sent its rolling thunder echoing up the cañon of the street. In a split second Lee was moving. He scooped up two fistfuls of dust and whipped them into Baldy's face as he lunged for the walk. He left his feet and hit the badman in a rolling dive. They went down together, Lee on top. His right fist arced down in a chopping blow that glanced off Baldy's jaw. A moment later, with the superhuman strength of liquor-toughened muscles, Baldy squirmed out from under and came to his feet.

The man forgot his weapons momentarily, and swung a booted foot at Lee, trying to rake him with a spur. But half a hundred prison fights had made Lee wary; he saw it coming; he twisted out of the way and reached up to catch the boot, and yank it.

In the two-second interval that caught Baldy off balance, Lee got his feet under him and cocked his fist. Suddenly his high-built body unfolded like a coiled spring. Baldy couldn't dodge, and the blow snapped his head back, lifting the man off his feet and sending him falling backwards. He hit the boardwalk in a driving skid that left him spread-eagled, with his hands groping for his fallen guns.

Lee stepped around him and took a tight hold on his shirt

front and heaved him to his feet. He stood there, glaring into the blank pale blue eyes for a second, and then drawled: "Never kick a man, Baldy. Don't ever do that to me again."

Baldy growled and feebly tried to break away. Then Lee released him. Baldy's knees gave way and he abruptly knelt on the walk, and then toppled sideways to lie without moving a muscle.

The crowd formed five seconds later, ringing the pair. Lee looked up in time to see the throng give way before the paunch pushing forward of a breathless man who wore a sheriff's badge. The lawman stepped within the circle and looked down at Baldy's inert form, and then back at Lee again, smiling broadly.

"I'm obliged for that, stranger. This gent's been on the prod in there for three hours. There ain't a man in town had the guts to go in and get him, me included."

He paused to wipe his perspiring forehead with a bandanna, then reached into a pocket and brought out a pair of handcuffs. "First time I've used 'em in close onto three years," he muttered as he stooped down to snap them over Baldy's wrists. He straightened up to say to the rest: "A couple of you carry him across to the jail. We'll let him sleep it off." He glanced at Lee once more, and added: "Goddlemighty, you sure pack a Sunday wallop, stranger."

Lee pushed out through the group of men and started down the walk. The Catamount would be crowded now, and he wanted nothing so much as his own company. He had gone half the distance to the saloon three doors below, when he saw his gelding being ridden in toward him to the hitch rail.

A girl was in the saddle, a girl who wore a man's faded blue Levi's and a tan cotton shirt open at the throat. Lee's bewilderment at seeing her astride the dun was overridden by an even greater surprise at her startling good looks. She was tall, with tawny hair and hazel eyes, and her deeply tanned face was so regular-featured that he immediately tried to find a flaw in its makeup, and couldn't.

"He's yours, isn't he?" the girl asked pleasantly, looking down at him. "I caught him for you. Everyone else was watching the fight. What happened?"

Before Lee could answer, a bass voice behind him boomed out: "Plenty happened! Mister, let me shake your hand!"

Lee turned to face a man almost as tall as himself, a man whose wide, heavy frame stood straightly erect despite his years, which Lee guessed to number close onto fifty. His grizzled, square-jawed countenance was set in a broad smile, where wide-spaced eyes, the same hazel shade of the girl's, now regarded Lee in sober admiration. He stretched out a hand, and Lee took it, feeling the firmness of the sure grasp.

"Climb down, Ellen," the man said, speaking to the girl. "Did you say you missed it? It was a pretty sight. Stranger, I admire a man who can settle his differences without burnin' powder."

The girl swung lightly out of the saddle and stepped up onto the walk beside the man. He put an arm about her shoulder and told Lee: "This is my daughter Ellen, stranger. My handle's Kinnard . . . Tom Kinnard."

Lee touched the brim of his Stetson in acknowledgment of the introduction. For the moment his thoughts centered on the girl and he smiled genuinely, his eyes for the moment lacking the hardness that invariably lay behind them. But suddenly the mention of that name struck a familiar chord in his memory and the smile faded.

He said soberly: "I'm Lee Anders."

"Anders?" A little of the warmth went out of Tom Kinnard's look. "So you finally drifted in," he said, appraising Lee a little more closely now. After a moment he glanced down at the girl and explained: "This is the man we were talking about this mornin', Ellen."

"From Yuma," Lee put in flatly.

"Some good men have come out of Yuma, Anders," the rancher said. "I may as well be frank and tell you I've studied your case. It's my opinion that you were the victim of circumstance. That's why I had you paroled to me."

"That's why you took my guns away?"

"I lost my faith in guns years ago," Kinnard answered, a little proudly. "I've put my own away and lived respectably since. No man with his share of guts needs to carry hardware. What you just did proves that."

"I was lucky, Kinnard. It didn't prove a thing."

The girl's glance had taken on a deeper shade of interest. Lee was feeling an unreasoning anger over the circumstance that had informed her of his true identity, but then he realized that it would have come to this eventually, and told himself it didn't matter. From now on these two would look on him as a specimen with which to experiment; he had been foolish a moment ago in thinking it could be otherwise.

Tom Kinnard, seeing the way his daughter looked at Lee, found something in her glance that was troubling. His grizzled face took on a lowering frown and he broke the awkward silence to say hastily: "We'll be startin' for home in a few minutes, Ellen. You'd better go tell Ollie to hitch up the team right away."

The girl nodded to Lee, and with a smile started across the street. Lee watched her with an oddly pleasurable excitement momentarily wiping out his regret. There was a certain carefree jauntiness in her swinging stride that fit the frankly open way she had regarded him. Remembering that, he instantly recognized Tom Kinnard's reason for sending her on this errand.

"You're careful of the company she keeps," he drawled.

Surprisingly enough, Tom Kinnard nodded. "I am," he said emphatically. "And I'll thank you to remember it while you're working for me."

Lee had expected Kinnard to be something like this, and now he bridled his rising irritation and even felt a faint amusement at the man's directness. "When do I start work?"

"Tonight or tomorrow . . . any time you feel like it."

"And if I find another job?"

Kinnard shrugged his shoulders disinterestedly. "So long as you keep your parole, it doesn't matter much where you work." Then with an attempt at affability: "Let's not get started wrong on this, Anders. I'm anxious to see you settle down and become a respected citizen again. Your secret's safe with me and my daughter. I haven't even told Ralph Moore, the sheriff. You're on your own now, and I want to see you make the best of it."

"I will," Lee told him. "Give me a day or two to hunt a job. I play hunches, Kinnard. And my hunch right now is that I'd rather work for someone else."

Half an hour later Lee was at the bar of the Catamount when the sheriff elbowed up alongside. He remembered Kinnard's telling him that the lawman's name was Ralph Moore, and gave him a civil greeting.

"The drinks are on me," Moore said good-naturedly. "Harry, slide us down a bottle."

The barkeep brought a bottle and two glasses, and Moore poured the drinks. He raised his glass: "Here's to cooler weather, stranger."

He was plainly uncomfortable, for the day was hot. Lee guessed his weight at two hundred and fifty; this, on a short frame that reached only to Lee's shoulder, made the man fat and shapeless. He took another drink of whiskey, and wiped his perspiring face and looked at Lee.

"There's something I'd like to talk over with you, stranger. Would you mind stepping across to my office?"

Lee nodded immediately, curious. They went out of the saloon and across the street to an end door in the sprawling adobe jail. Moore entered first, and, stepping in after him, Lee found himself in the presence of three other men who regarded his entrance with undisguised interest.

"Here he is, gents," the sheriff announced to the trio. "Now it's your turn." He named them off to Lee: "This is Earl Semple, stranger, and over there is Ben Fields. The other is Elmer Dryden. They're the town commissioners."

Semple, the one sitting in the sheriff's swivel chair behind the scarred desk, appeared to be the leader. He was a handsome man, outfitted in a black suit and an immaculately laundered white shirt. Just now he cleared his throat nervously, and began: "This is a little irregular, stranger, but we wanted a talk with you. The fact is, we all saw the fight across the street and liked the way you handled it. We. . . ."

"Hell, Earl!" the sheriff interrupted. "Talk straight! Stranger, these gents have been lookin' for a new marshal. They think you fit the bill. Will you or won't you?"

"Will I what?" Lee asked, confused by the sheriff's bluntness.

"Will you take the job of town marshal?" Semple put in.

A heavy silence settled over the room. It took Lee a few seconds to catch the full significance of what they were asking. Then suddenly he laughed softly, amused at the irony of the thing. Lee Anders, fresh from Yuma, serving out his parole behind a law badge.

Hearing that mocking laughter, Ben Fields, a wizened old man with a perpetually set scowl on his leathery visage, looked up sharply and growled: "It's a fair enough offer. The job pays a hundred a month."

Lee nodded, sobering once more. "It is a fair offer. But I can't take it."

"Why not?" This from the sheriff.

160

"I'm no lawman. I don't even carry hardware. But what I would like is a riding job for one of the outfits around here."

Semple's black eyes took on a new light. "Then you are looking for work?"

"Sure. I'll take anything. Anything but your marshal's badge."

"That settles it," Semple said, slapping the desk top with his open palm. He glanced over at the sheriff. "Ralph, you tell him."

The sheriff shook his head stubbornly. "This wasn't my idea, Earl. You're halfway along, so now you finish it."

Lee was puzzled at what meaning lay behind this exchange of words. He didn't have to wait long for his explanation, for Semple looked back at him once more. He said levelly: "We won't take no for an answer, stranger. Either take the job we're offering, or we'll have Moore put you under arrest."

"Arrest?" Lee echoed incredulously. "How could you frame that?"

"There's an old city ordinance we haven't used for years that makes a man liable to arrest for street brawling. We can dig it out and use it, an', by God, we will."

Lee caught on at last. "You call what happened out there a brawl?"

"We'll call it that if we have to," came Semple's answer. "Stranger, we don't aim to be hard on you, but we need a marshal. You can take care of any trouble that comes along. I don't know why you won't carry guns, but that's not important. You don't need 'em from the looks of things."

Lee held back the hot retort that instinctively flashed through his mind. Under any other circumstances this threat wouldn't have mattered. But now, out on parole and good behavior, even that arrest would carry with it the red tape and legal machinery that might mean the canceling of his parole. These men didn't know this; they were making this play in the hope that they could bluff him. There was another thing to be considered, too. Here was the job he had been wishing for, work that would take him out from under Tom Kinnard's watchful eye. He hadn't been impressed by Kinnard. The man was all right, probably, but a little too straight-laced to suit Lee. There seemed only one way out.

"You couldn't make an arrest stick," he taunted them, speaking mainly to Earl Semple. "But I won't put you to the trouble of trying. I'll take your badge."

II

They fined Baldy Mason $100 and let him out of jail the following afternoon. Lee purposely avoided him, and two hours later watched him ride out the west trail.

He felt an immediate relief, for he had been uneasy with Baldy in town. He knew that the years in Yuma had changed the man from a petty gunman and thief to a hardcase killer, and he had no wish to let it get around that he knew him. These people weren't acquainted with the man, yet two hundred miles north it was legend that wherever Baldy Mason rode, there rode trouble. And Lee was for steering shy of trouble if it was possible. But that night, eating his supper at the lunch counter in the Catamount, he experienced a sudden foreboding at sight of Baldy, coming in through the swing doors up front, heading directly back to the lunch counter.

Lee turned his head, hoping to escape recognition, but Baldy sauntered up, took the stool alongside.

"Well, if it ain't Lee Anders, pride of the Yuma broom shop," he drawled.

Lee turned slowly to face him. "Would you like that nose busted over again, Baldy, or should I put another lump on your jaw?"

Baldy chuckled. "I ain't holdin' that against you, Anders.

Maybe I had it comin', and you sure did a swell job on me. How drunk was I?"

"What's on your mind?" Lee asked with sudden directness.

The gunman shrugged his heavy sloping shoulders. "Nothin' much. How long you been out?" He had pushed his Stetson onto the back of his head so that his hairless scalp caught the lamplight and shone like a well-polished cue ball. His pale blue eyes were a trifle bloodshot from the aftereffects of his drunk the day before, and on the left side of his blunt, unshaven chin showed a sizeable lump at the spot where Lee's fist had struck him. He wore two guns in holsters riding low on his thighs. He wasn't pretty.

"I've been out twelve days," Lee told him.

"And the badge?" the gunman queried significantly.

"They wished that on me when I rode in here. No one but my parole officer knows where I came from. He won't tell 'em . . . and neither will you."

Again Baldy gave that careless shrug of his shoulders. "Why should I spoil your play? Not me."

Lee sensed that Baldy was leading up to something.

"And without guns, too," he added.

"Sage City's a peaceful town, Baldy."

A look of cunning edged Baldy's glance for a fleeting instant, and then his eyes went unreadable once more.

"I was thinkin' the same. Peaceful . . . and prosperous." He hesitated so that Lee could weigh the meaning that backed his words. "Prosperous, feller. We could fix that if we worked it right."

Lee laid down his knife and fork and turned to the gunman. "Maybe you ought to be leaving, Baldy," he said softly. "Maybe you even ought to pile onto your hull and rag it out of town!"

Baldy sat there a few seconds longer before he edged back off the stool to stand, spraddle-legged, regarding Lee. His long arms hung ape-like, close to his guns, and his thick lips curled down into a sneer. "So it's that way, is it?"

Lee came to his feet with a careless ease that put him within reach of the other. "Yeah . . . just that way, hardcase. Do you want to make anything of it?"

The man's sneer held and his pale blue eyes went cloudy with anger as he said: "You're makin' big medicine for a man with so little to back it, friend."

"Try me, Baldy. Try me."

For a long moment Baldy appeared undecided. Then his shifty eyes fell before Lee's hard scrutiny, and finally he faced about and walked slowly toward the doors up front. He turned and flashed a look back at Lee before he stepped out, and in that one glance Lee found something that immediately brought up a foreboding of things to come. . . .

It was an hour later when the shouts echoed from far down the street. The bar emptied quickly, and Lee followed the others out through the swing doors. A man came running down the walk yelling—"Fire!"—and with that cry the walks became a milling mass of humanity that surged steadily along the street. A rosy glow of light tinted the dark sky ahead at the far end of town. A quarter minute later, as Lee was running along the walk with the crowd, the tank wagon of Sage City's fire brigade rattled past in a boiling cloud of dust, the four horses that pulled it lunging in a mad gallop.

Earl Semple's big frame house was afire. The square, two-story structure was a mass of flames by the time Lee arrived to help hold the crowd back. Men formed a bucket line from the tank wagon to the house, but there was little use in bringing water when no one could get close enough to the roaring flames to empty the buckets.

Earl Semple and his wife were two of the last arrivals. They had been spending the evening with friends at the other end of town. No, they didn't know how the fire could have started, for they hadn't left even a lamp burning.

Later, shortly after the walls toppled inward to send a huge plume of flame shooting skyward, a drunkenly weaving figure came up the street toward the fringe of the crowd. It was Ben Fields. He was in close before his choking cries rose above the sound of the crackling flames.

Lee, turning at the sound of that hoarse voice, was one of the first to reach him. Fields's forehead was streaked with blood, and a large lump showed high up on his scalp as he staggered into the light of the burning house.

"The store!" Fields croaked. "The money's gone! Over two thousand dollars!"

He paused breathlessly, looking about him, wild-eyed, finally to single Lee out of the crowd. He reached up to wipe the blood out of his eyes, then glared at Lee and said bitingly: "Well, where was you, Anders? Where's the protection we got when we hired you? This is the first time in ten years we've had a robbery."

Finally they quieted him enough so that he could tell a coherent story. "I was workin' late over the account books," he explained. "Of course, I heard about the fire. I went out and looked up the street at it, but I wasn't goin' kid crazy over a big blaze. I went back to work. It was maybe five minutes later when I heard a board creak behind me. As I turned to take a look, somethin' banged down on my head and knocked me out. That's the last I knew until five minutes ago. I found the safe open, an' every damned cent in it was gone! Twenty-one hundred and forty dollars!" One bony finger pointed accusingly at Lee. "And yesterday we hired us a marshal!"

Lee took the scathing remark in silence. Then, as soon as he could get away, he edged out to the limits of the crowd and listened to what was being said. He wanted to think.

With the fire starting so mysteriously along with the store robbery, a single idea took hold of Lee. Baldy Mason was back of this. It was like him to play it slick like that, dragging every soul in town from the place he had planned to rob.

Lee looked about him with little hope of finding Baldy. By now the man would be on his horse and miles away from Sage City. But as he glanced around, he saw Baldy halfway down the bucket line, working with the rest, his Stetson off, his bald head shining in the orange light of the flames, and his blue denim shirt sweat-streaked, as he passed on bucket after bucket.

For long seconds, Lee doubted the wisdom of his decision. But finally he walked over to the line and in behind Baldy. He reached out and lifted Baldy's two .45s from their holsters before the man even knew of his presence.

Baldy passed on the bucket in his right hand and stepped back out of the line. His unshaven face twisted into an ugly look as he turned and recognized Lee.

"What's the play, tin star?" he queried.

"You're under arrest for starting this fire, Baldy."

The gunman grinned and shook his head: "You can't make it stick, Marshal. You can't make it stick."

Twenty minutes later, in the sheriff's office, Lee and Ben Fields and Earl Semple and three others confronted the prisoner.

"Then you don't recognize him?" Lee asked Fields, whose head was now wrapped in a crude bandage.

"How the hell could I?" the storekeeper growled, his gaunt face set in its perpetual scowl. "I tell you all I saw was a shadow."

"And you claim this man was at the fire from the time it started?" Lee asked one of the others.

The man he addressed shifted his feet nervously and gave an eloquent shrug. "That's pinning me down too close, Marshal.

All I said was that I saw this gent when I got to the fire. Things was too lively to notice much. As far as I know, he was there all the time. He got in line when we tried to water the fire the first time, and he was there to give a hand when the walls fell in and gave us a hand with the buckets later on."

"Then he could have left without your noticing?"

"Sure." The man grinned. "I wasn't follerin' him."

Lee frowned wearily and looked across at Baldy, who sat on one corner of the sheriff's desk with a cigarette drooping from one side of his mouth.

Baldy caught the pointed scrutiny, and said: "You can't hang this on me, friend. Lock me up and I'll hire the best lawyer in the county to snake me out. I'll come back with my own crowd, an' we'll show you how to bust a town wide open. We'll wipe it off the map."

Earl Semple put in his word now. He was irritable and quarrelsome because of the loss of his house, but Lee had sensed the man's open dislike for him ever since this group had gathered here.

"You're makin' fools of the bunch of us, Anders," the banker complained. "It's my idea you're workin' off a grudge against this man. He was drunk the other day and actin' up some, but that don't make him liable for everything that goes wrong."

"Then you want me to let him go?" Lee asked narrowly. "What about you, Sheriff?"

Moore shifted his bulk a little deeper to his swivel chair and shook his head resignedly: "You heard what he said. He can make it damned hot for us, unless we got evidence."

"All right, Baldy," Lee said finally. "You can go. But by tomorrow night be clear of this town. As long as I wear this badge, you'll keep outside the town limits."

"That's puttin' it a little stiff, isn't it?" Earl Semple asked, quick to jump to Baldy's defense because of his dislike for Lee.

"That's for me to say," was Lee's answer. "You've given me this badge and that's my order."

Semple eyed him for a long moment and said pointedly: "It might be in line for you to resign, Anders."

Lee smiled wryly, and shook his head. "Not any, mister. You dealt me this hand and now I'm playing it out to the last chip."

III

The next afternoon Tom Kinnard was in town. Lee met the rancher as he was coming out of the bank at closing time.

"So you found a job?" Kinnard said, nodding his satisfaction as he glanced down at the marshal's badge. "That's fine. You ought to make a good officer, Anders."

"There's some that don't agree with you. Last night I was asked to resign. I may be out after that other job soon."

"That'll blow over," Kinnard assured him. "I've had a talk with Earl Semple. He's satisfied, and so is Ben Fields. The only thing they didn't like was your rawhidin' this man Mason. Why did you do it?"

"He was in Yuma with me. I know him. He's plenty mean."

"Just because he's been in Yuma?"

"No, not that," Lee answered. "Yuma didn't have much to do with making Baldy what he is."

Kinnard considered this. Then: "Don't be too hard on the man, Anders. Remember that he's in the same boat you are. Give him his chance the same as we're givin' you yours."

His words brought up a quick light of anger to Lee's gray eyes. Seeing it and understanding what he had done, Kinnard was about to offer an apology. But before he could speak, Lee was drawling: "I hadn't looked at it that way, Kinnard. I reckon we're a couple of strays. Thanks . . . for remindin' me!" And he sauntered off down the walk.

Ellen Kinnard, watching from the seat of her father's

buckboard across the street, saw Lee walk away from her father.

Tom Kinnard came across and climbed up beside her in silence, backing his team of big bays out from the rail and sending them on down the street at a smart trot. He had carried a bulging saddlebag across from the bank and now laid it on the seat beside him; it contained nearly $400, the monthly payroll for his cowpunchers.

"What did he have to say?" Ellen asked as the last scattered adobes of the town fell behind along the road.

Tom Kinnard gave her a mildly quizzical look. "Who?"

"Your man from Yuma."

The rancher frowned. "You interested in him, Ellen?"

The girl's oval face colored at the question and she turned her head so that he couldn't catch her momentary confusion. "Interested? No, no more than in anyone else."

"He's not your kind, honey," Kinnard went on, disregarding her denial. "The man is hard as granite. I can remember the days when I admired his kind. But I've learned better."

"He seemed quite nice."

Tom Kinnard's low chuckle was tinged with sobriety as he said: "They're all nice, until they run into trouble. Then, if a gun's handy, they turn into killers."

"Dad!" the girl cried reproachfully. "You've no right to say that! Why, you carried guns yourself for years. You made your name by them."

Then all at once she regretted her words. She hadn't meant to come to Lee Anders's defense, but her father had caught her unaware. After all, this man Anders was a paroled criminal and was being dealt with in the way he deserved. She had heard about his appointment as marshal, and the fact that he carried no guns had indefinably troubled her.

She tried to put down her interest in him, yet the vaguely disturbing warm light that had come into his eyes the other day at sight of her remained a clear picture in her mind. She hadn't forgotten it, nor yet did she understand it, even now. But that was no reason for defending him, so now she looked up at her father and said: "I'm sorry, Dad."

To Tom Kinnard, Lee was the visual embodiment of what he himself had been twenty years ago. Ellen's words had set him to thinking, and for the first time in years he put down the prejudices he had built up and calmly asked himself if he wasn't being a little too severe toward Anders.

Ahead, the line of Five Mile Ridge crept slowly toward them, until at length the road angled to meet the ridge at its lowest point. Soon they began the climb that would take them over the crest. Up there, the trail cut in between two high shoulders of massive rock, and beyond there it headed once more across level country.

The team was five rods short of the rim when the sharp, flat *crash* of a rifle sounded out above the *rattle* of the wheels and the *creak* of harness leather. A bullet whined overhead in sudden warning. Tom Kinnard reined in on the team, threw on the brake, and pulled Ellen in behind him with one powerful sweep of his arm.

His searching glance ran on above the trail, inspecting the rock ledges that butted it. He caught sight of a drifting cloud of powder smoke. An instant later a gruff voice shouted down: "Throw down that money!"

In another second, Kinnard spied the crown of a Stetson showing from behind a massive boulder above. He hesitated an instant, considering his chance of turning the team and heading back down the trail. But there was no room to turn here, and they were close enough to be a sure target for the man above.

Then sudden anger loosed itself in Kinnard. His two big hands opened and closed in a gesture that was at once helpless and eloquent. He longed to feel the butt of a gun in his palm.

He cursed and growled to Ellen: "Stay set. I'll get us out of this." Then, in a louder voice, he called: "What money?"

In answer, a second shot ripped away the silence, and this time the slug *slapped* into the dust ahead of the team. One of the bays shied nervously toward the edge of the trail.

Tom Kinnard was a sensible man. He did the only sensible thing under these circumstances. He reached down and lifted the saddlebag off the seat and tossed it out into the dust alongside the trail.

"Now get goin'!" came the second sharp command from above.

As Kinnard sat straight in the seat once more, and rein-slapped the team to start them on up the slope, he searched his memory for recognition of that voice. Finally, as they topped the ridge and rattled off down the road at a faster clip, he decided that he had never heard it before.

For the better part of a mile he drove fast and in a belligerent silence. Then he glanced down at his daughter to find her smiling at him with a brightly amused light in her hazel eyes.

"What is it?" he asked gruffly.

"I was only thinking that a gun would have come in handy back there. After all, four hundred dollars is four hundred dollars."

"He was hidden," Kinnard snapped. "No man could have got to him for a shot."

"There was a time, years ago, when you'd have tried it, Dad," Ellen said in a mildly accusing tone. "It ought to prove to you that there's a time and a place for everything, guns included."

He had no answer for that. Nor did she press her point, but sat quietly beside him with that faint smile lingering at the corners of her lips.

Ten minutes later Kinnard abruptly stopped the team and

wheeled them around to head back along the road. Still Ellen said nothing. When they came to the ridge and started down the incline, Kinnard reined in and got down without a word of explanation.

He climbed up to the point where he glimpsed the crown of that gray Stetson and started examining the rock crevices behind the boulder. Soon he found what he was looking for, two empty brass shells. He examined them carefully, noting their caliber and the markings of the firing pin. "Winchester Thirty-Thirty," he muttered. "About as much help as a wet match in a blizzard."

Down below once again, he walked on along the trail to where he had thrown out the saddlebag. There, showing clearly in the sandy soil, were three hoof prints. He studied them carefully, and, when Ellen drove alongside, he straightened and told her soberly: "We'll drive back to town and have a look. I'll know that sign if I see it again."

When they drove down Sage City's street an hour later, the sun had dipped out of sight over the horizon behind and given way to quick-settling twilight. Kinnard made for the livery barn. Inside, he found Ollie Humphreys, owner of the stable, and asked him: "Who's been in or out over the past two hours, Ollie?"

Humphreys pushed his hat off his forehead and ran his fingers through his thatch of red hair. "Three or four, Tom. Doc Parrish rode away sometime about three. Before him went that Mason gent. He was gone until about ten or fifteen minutes ago. Bob Rue was in and out a couple of times, and Fred Nichols took his. . . ."

"Is Mason's horse here now?" Kinnard interrupted.

Ollie nodded disinterestedly. "You'll find him in the back stall. I got work to do, Tom. Help yourself."

Kinnard went on back to the last stall and around to the

front of it to untie the big roan gelding's halter rope. He led the animal out of the stable and into the corral lot out back, and walked him halfway across and back again to the stall where he retied him. Once in the corral again and stooping over the tracks the roan had made, even the poor light was good enough to give him his answer. These hoof prints matched those he had seen out by Five Mile Ridge.

He went out front and climbed into the buckboard again and sent the team back up the street. As he pulled over to the hitch rail in front of the jail, Ellen asked: "Was Lee Anders right?"

"Right about what?"

"Was it Baldy Mason?"

Kinnard nodded. "He's the one that got our payroll. I don't know about the other robbery." He climbed down and started out across the walk.

"I'm coming with you, Dad," Ellen said, stepping down from the seat and following him.

Both Lee and the sheriff were in the office as Tom and Ellen entered.

Moore looked at Kinnard in surprise and said: "Back so soon, Tom?"

Kinnard told them his story briefly, omitting nothing. He told about finding the sign and checking it with that of Baldy Mason's roan gelding.

When he had finished, Lee sat quietly regarding him for the space of several seconds. Then he nodded briefly, and got up off his chair and said: "So it's up to me again, is it?"

Kinnard said: "Someone's got to make the arrest."

An unspoken thought brought a faint smile to Lee's lean face. He opened his hands and rubbed his palms along his thighs, and looked first at Kinnard, and then at the girl, and drawled: "Whatever you say goes. Baldy's across the street. I reckon he's expecting me."

"You're . . . you're not going after him . . . unarmed?" Ellen queried as Lee stepped to the door.

"No man with his share of guts needs to carry hardware," Lee told her, repeating the words Tom Kinnard had used on their first meeting.

The girl remembered, and her face took on a deep flush as she met Lee's level glance. Then he was gone out the door. As his steps faded down the walk, the girl shot her father an imploring look. The rancher purposely avoided meeting his daughter's glance.

IV

The Catamount was crowded for this time of evening, the supper hour. For the word had made the rounds that Baldy Mason had overstayed his time limit in town, and men were here waiting to see what the new marshal would do about it. Bets were being taken at three-to-one odds that Anders wouldn't come after Mason.

Baldy stood alone at the end of the bar, his back to the wall, his eyes peering unwinkingly through the orange-blue smoke haze toward the doors. Men were careful to keep out of the line between the gunman and the doors, so that when Lee brushed the batwings aside and stepped in he had a clear view of the man he was seeking.

Baldy's flat-nosed face took on a smile as he sighted Lee. He shoved out from the bar and waited. A sudden silence filled the room; men stepped far back out of the way, and it was as though Lee and Baldy had the place to themselves.

Then Lee came straight down the length of the bar until he was within eight feet of Baldy.

The gunman growled: "No closer, friend."

Lee did a strange thing. He turned to Harry Rue, the barkeep, and drawled: "I'll have a bourbon."

Harry set a bottle and a glass on the bar and edged out of the way. "Another glass for my partner here," Lee told him.

Harry brought another glass. Lee poured himself a drink, and only then looked at Baldy. The gunman stood facing him, his left elbow on the bar top, his right thumb hooked in his belt close to his gun.

"Will we have a drink before we settle this?" Lee asked him.

"Why not?" came Baldy's confident answer. "Where's your irons, Marshal?"

"I thought you knew I couldn't carry 'em," Lee told him. Then, in a gesture that was as casual as it was natural, he took hold of the bottle and abruptly sent it sliding down the bar toward Baldy, saying: "Pour your own."

The move took Baldy by surprise. Instinctively he brought his right hand up to stop the bottle from hitting the wall. In the same split second Lee was moving. Baldy saw his mistake, let the bottle slide on past, and flashed his hand too late down toward his holster.

The bottle shattered against the wall just as Lee flipped Baldy's guns out of their holsters. He rocked them a moment in his palms as the gunman tensed, ready to spring at him. But as Baldy faced the menace of his own hair-triggered weapons, he lost his nerve and edged away. Seeing this, Lee stuck the weapons in the belt of his Levi's and drawled: "Will you come peaceful, or do you want the same thing I handed you the other afternoon?"

With a surly growl, Baldy stepped on past him and walked toward the doors.

Across the street in the jail office, Baldy's entrance brought a frank stare of amazement to Sheriff Ralph Moore's round face. Ellen Kinnard glanced on past the gunman and spied Lee. She looked immediately relieved and happy, while her father's eyes lighted up. "I knew you'd do it, Anders." He grinned.

"Lock him up, Sheriff," Lee said curtly, laying Baldy's guns on the desk. "You'd better search him for hide-outs."

"Where did you cache the money?" Moore snapped out, stepping over to Baldy.

"Try and find it," was Baldy's surly answer.

Moore chuckled and said: "We'll beat it out of you, brother!" He reached out and ran his hands around Baldy's waist, feeling for a hidden weapon. For a brief moment the lawman stood between Baldy and Lee, and in that instant Lee saw the gunman's fist dart down to snatch one of Moore's guns from its holster.

Before any of them could make a move, Baldy dodged away from the sheriff and swung the short-barreled .45 to cover them. Then he reached out and took Ellen by the wrist and pulled her toward him.

"Don't one of you move. The girl goes with me while I saddle and ride out of here. I may take her with me a ways. If you want her back safe, stay set, gents."

Ellen's frightened cry was in Lee's ears, as Baldy backed out the door and pulled her after him, the .45 still leveled. Then he and the girl edged out of sight, and the three in the office heard them run down the boardwalk.

Tom Kinnard took a step toward the door, but Lee reached out and stopped him. "I'd take his word for it, Kinnard. He said to stay set," Lee drawled.

"Do something, one of you!" Kinnard roared savagely. "Don't stand here and let him get away with this!"

"Do what?" Lee said softly, holding out his two hands. "What can I do with these? I've corralled that curly wolf twice for you with these bare hands. Now you want me to go after him again? Hell, you're loco, Kinnard."

"Ralph, he's on his way to the stable after his roan," Kinnard said desperately to the sheriff. "Get on down there and stop him!"

Sheriff Moore, pale and shaking, shook his head. "Not me, Tom. This is out o' my line. It's the marshal's job. That jasper's too salty for me to handle. He'll send Ellen back when he gets good and ready. Not before."

Suddenly a change came over Tom Kinnard. He grew calm as he looked at Lee once more and asked in a level voice: "Will you go after him, Anders? Will you, if I'll give you a pair of guns?"

Without answer, Lee went over to lift one of Baldy Mason's six-guns off the desk. He thumbed back the hammer and tested the trigger pull. It was light as a feather. His gray eyes had taken on a new look, a sudden hardness that made Tom Kinnard watch instead of talk.

Without a word, Lee left the office and ran down the walk toward the stable. He cut between two buildings, and ran back to the alley that would put him alongside the stable corral.

A quarter minute later he was crawling between the poles of the corral, and making for the open maw of the livery stable's rear door that loomed up out of the darkness ahead. There was a faint glow of light showing from inside as he walked silently up to the opening.

Stepping out so that he could look down the length of the barn, he spied Baldy. The gunman was holding a weapon lined at Ollie Humphreys, who was nervously saddling the roan. Ellen stood to one side of Baldy, her oval face pale with fright, but her hazel eyes showing a defiant look.

"Hurry it!" Baldy snarled at Ollie as Lee stepped nearer.

Ollie's jerky movements quickened as he stooped to reach under the roan's belly for the cinch.

At that instant, Lee called out softly: "Have a look back here, Baldy."

The gunman whirled, jerking the girl in front of him, and swiveling up his Colt, his close-set eyes searching the shadows beyond the door.

Lee thumbed back the hammer of his weapon once and sent a shot thundering into the barn loft. Baldy saw the gun flash and ripped out two roaring blasts in answer. That was what Lee wanted.

As the thunder of Baldy's gun cut loose, he was moving to the other side of the door, hoping to get Ellen's body out of line of fire and no longer shielding the gunman.

When he was in position, he stepped into the light.

Baldy caught sight of him and made a frantic effort to swing his gun around. But in that fraction of a second Lee fired. Baldy screamed as the bullet shattered his wrist. The heavy .45 fell from his big hand to spin to the floor.

Ellen twisted away from him and kicked the gun farther out of reach, and then Lee Anders was in close. He tossed his weapon aside and swung one short blow. It caught Baldy on the ear, and Baldy went down.

Tom Kinnard and the sheriff ran in through the front door of the stable seconds later. They found Ellen in Lee's arms, her head on his shoulder, sobbing brokenly as she gave way to her fright. Ollie Humphrey knelt over the unconscious Baldy nearby, doing his best at bandaging the man's shattered wrist with his bandanna.

Kinnard grinned when he saw his daughter safe. As he approached the pair, Lee pushed the girl away from him in confused embarrassment, and held out the gun in his hand, saying: "I don't reckon I'll need this any more, Kinnard."

"Keep it," Tom answered. "It'll do you until we drive out home. I never thought I'd unpack my pair of silver-mounted Thirty-Eights again, but I'm goin' to! They're yours, Anders. How about that job I offered you?"

Before Lee could give his reply, Ellen spoke: "Maybe, if you put him on as foreman. . . ."

Kinnard's countenance broke into a smile. He nodded, and finally turned to the sheriff. "Ellen knows damn' well I never hire an unmarried man to rod my outfit," he said.

★ ★ ★ ★ ★

Posse Guns

★ ★ ★ ★ ★

Jon Glidden was writing many stories in 1937. He and his wife Dorothy were faced with a major decision. Jon's brother, Fred Glidden, who wrote Western fiction under the name Luke Short, and his wife had moved out of Santa Fé and settled in Pojoaque Valley, near Los Alamos, and Fred was now urging his brother to join him there. Jonathan and Dorothy decided that they should give full-time writing a try for three months, to see if he could earn the $200 a month they estimated it would cost to survive in New Mexico. The gamble paid off. Jonathan produced nine stories in a two-month period, and just two of these brought in more than the necessary $200. In the spring of 1937 they moved to Pojoaque where, for $1,000, they bought a nine-room adobe house, across the road from where Fred and his wife lived. This story, one of the many Jon wrote that year, was titled "Fast Guns Blaze Against the King Bolt." It was sold to Leo Margulies at Standard Magazines on December 7, 1937 for $90. The title was changed to "Posse Guns" when it appeared in *Popular Western* (7/38), the only Peter Dawson story ever to appear in any magazine from this publisher. It was subsequently reprinted as "Posse Guns" in *Thrilling Ranch Stories* (Fall, 50). The magazine title has been retained for its appearance here.

I

It was a clannish country, this Sawtooth range. Even now, riding alongside Deputy Sheriff Bert Welch, Joe Dorn felt that they hadn't accepted him. On and off for the past two years they'd called on him for things like this, to help out, but that meant nothing. Today there would be strangers in the posse, men commandeered by the law to do a public service, and he would be treated as one of the strangers.

"How did it happen?" he asked, as he looked across at the deputy.

Bert Welch, massive of figure and deliberate of speech, answered evasively.

"Some tell it one way, some another. You'd better wait and git the story straight from the sheriff. Anyhow, Ray Temple's dead."

Dorn's lean face and gray eyes reflected a trace of amusement. Riding with another man, Welch would have been his usual talkative self, full of the details of the tragedy responsible for the gathering of the posse.

The deputy spurred his short-legged gelding obviously in a hurry to end this ride. He had been sent from town to gather men from the three outfits that lay at the base of the foothills. Joe Dorn was the only available man he had found, however, the others being at work high in the snow-mantled foothills. And Dan Morgan, Dorn's partner, was away, too.

Dorn hadn't been able to explain Morgan's absence to the

deputy. He wasn't sure where Morgan had gone. In the two years of their partnership, Morgan had often disappeared like this for days at a time, and Dorn had never questioned him. They were old friends, but Dan Morgan's business was his own.

They had made a good combination. Morgan's money had bought the layout and Dorn's experience had made it a paying proposition. Their roundup had netted 2,300 head this fall and there was money in the bank under Joe Dorn's name—all in two years.

Dorn and the deputy made the Split Diamond at 9:00 a.m. A knot of horsemen was gathered in the front yard, twenty-three men from all the valley outfits. Ren Bolt was there, with half a dozen of his King Bolt crew.

It was Bolt who took Joe Dorn's eye as he drew rein with a casual. " 'Mornin', men." Invariably he felt a flare of antagonism whenever he saw Ken Bolt—and Bolt had always made his own dislike pretty obvious. The King Bolt owner's leggy blue stallion was ground-hitched at the porch steps, and the tall, heavy man was talking to Helen Norris.

Joe Dorn thought he caught a faint welcoming smile on her flawless features as she glanced at him, and as usual it was in his mind what a pleasing picture she made with her tawny hair and deep brown eyes and skin tanned to the color of turning oak leaves. Somehow it took away the sting of the other casual greetings to think that she really welcomed him, didn't stand coldly aloof like the rest.

Sheriff Bob Crawford came out with John Norris, the owner of the Split Diamond. Past fifty, both of them, yet age had robbed them of little of their vigor. Norris was tall, portly, grizzled. Crawford stood half a head shorter, was spare-bodied, and with only a rarely glimpsed hard glint coming to his honest brown eyes to hint of his iron will. His eyes flashed that granite-like quality now as he spoke to the gathered men.

"We'll work north and east into the hills, from there up Deep Gulch. You know what we'll find . . . a hundred places where a man might hide out and cut half of us to ribbons before we kin take cover. But we go in the whole way. Ray Temple's dead and that calls for more'n it did when it was only the loss of a few critters, like it's been before when we went up there. We're going to stamp out this wild bunch, so if any of you want to go on home, now's the time to do it."

No man moved. In the hush only the nervous *stamping* of a restless bronco and the creak of saddle leather sounded mutedly through the still air.

Suddenly Ren Bolt spoke: "How about Dorn, Sheriff?"

Crawford wheeled, and didn't see Joe Dorn swing out of his saddle and start for the porch.

"What about Dorn?" the lawman snapped. "He's one of us till he's proved different. That's a hell of a thing to say about any. . . ."

Sight of Joe Dorn's walking past cut short his words. Joe Dorn mounted the steps, not knowing the reasons for Bolt's remark, but certain the time for a showdown with this man had come. As he stepped close to Bolt, he looked a trifle shabby in his Levi's, blue cotton shirt, and faded vest compared with the King Bolt owner in his expensive black broadcloth trousers, gray flannel shirt, and skin-tight, shiny boots. Dorn was a shade taller than Bolt's six feet and his shoulders were wider, yet Bolt's massive shoulders and arms so greatly gave the impression of strength that he looked the bigger man.

Dorn's gray eyes were hard as deliberately he unbuckled his gun belt and swung it and his holstered Colts to the porch floor.

"I'll give you a chance to take it back, Bolt," he drawled softly. "Either that, or shed your irons. We'll have it out right here."

Hot anger flushed Ren Bolt's square-jawed face, then cunning crept into his eyes. He had started unbuckling the double belts that were weighed down by his two ivory-handled six-guns when John Norris's deep voice boomed out: "I'll have no brawl on my place! Ren, you . . . !"

But in that instant Bolt's right fist whipped up in an arcing blow that caught Joe Dorn alongside the jaw. A trick, since Bolt still wore one of his guns and the blow was unexpected. Dorn staggered backward, smashing into a roof pillar. With a startled cry, gazing unbelievingly at Bolt, Helen Norris shrank back.

Dorn shook his head to clear it. Bolt made a sudden rush and to the watchers it looked as if Joe Dorn was down again, for his attempt to dodge was a stagger. But that awkward lunge carried him out of reach of Bolt's swinging fists and an instant later, his head cleared, he faced the man again.

Half a hundred fights had schooled Joe Dorn in measuring a man. As Ren Bolt rushed in, he waited and took the first blow against his raised shoulder. Then, before Bolt's fist met its mark, all the weight and strength of Dorn's tall frame swung behind a fist that drove upward and smashed in below Bolt's breastbone. Bolt's lancing left lost its power as he doubled. Fast as light Dorn followed that first blow with two more, one to each side of the jaw, the second jerking Bolt's whole frame as his knees buckled.

He fell forward as if already unconscious. But Dorn, standing spraddle-legged over him, didn't take his eyes off that sprawled figure until Sheriff Crawford reached him, took him by the arm.

"You ride, Dorn," the sheriff said grimly. "It was fair and I'll back you. But get away from here and stay out of Ren's way. I won't have you two burning powder over this thing."

"What thing?" Joe Dorn asked quietly.

The sheriff shrugged as though hesitant to speak.

"I'm not saying it's true, Dorn, but it was two of Ren's King

Bolt riders that found Ray Temple this morning. Ray had followed the wild bunch back into Deep Gulch and it was there they found him. According to them, he talked before he cashed in, said he'd recognized Dan Morgan as one of the rustlers. But Ren was addle-headed when he tried to bring you in on it." Sternly he faced the group at the foot of the steps. "I say any man's a damn' fool to try to saddle Joe Dorn with this thing till it's proved on him! Till then, my word goes!"

"Do you believe it, Crawford?" Dorn asked tightly.

Again Crawford lifted his shoulders. "All I know is what I see. I haven't seen Morgan swinging his rope on any critter that doesn't carry his brand. After today mebbe I'll know more."

"I'd like to ride with you today," Dorn said soberly. "Maybe I'd learn a few things I don't know myself."

Crawford shook his head. "Ren will be along, Joe. You'd better ride on back home."

Riding along the trail that led toward the high foothills and his ranch, Joe Dorn's temper cooled enough to let him sanely consider what he had heard. To be accused by a dying man made it look bad for Dan Morgan. But Joe Dorn was troubled, doubtful. There were things he knew about Morgan that didn't fit with his being a rustler.

For one thing, Dan Morgan had money, plenty of it. His father had been one of the first one hundred at Virginia City, and had died leaving more than enough for his four children. It had been Morgan's whim to come here and buy the D Bar. And he had generously given Dorn half title to the small outfit in exchange for his knowledge of cattle.

They had kept to themselves, for Morgan preferred a solitary life. He had an aloofness that had made these people think him arrogant. But he was not like that with Joe Dorn, who had known him all his life. No, there was no reason for a man as honest as Dan Morgan to rustle another man's beef.

Maybe Ray Temple was seeing wrong, Dorn mused as his chestnut took the long grade to the top of a high ridge. *Maybe he didn't see Dan at all. Maybe he wasn't even alive when Bolt's riders found him.* But out of all the crowding ideas, one thought leaped to his mind and stayed. *What if Ren Bolt had framed this on Dan Morgan?*

Bolt had been the first to start the feeling against Morgan and Dorn two years ago. Plain enough why, for he had lost out when Morgan bought the land that bordered the King Bolt, paying the asking price for the brand, instead of stealing it from Tom Mason's widow as Bolt had tried to do.

But suddenly Dorn's reasoning hit a stumbling block when he remembered Dan Morgan's mysterious trips. Those times Morgan was away from the D Bar did fit in with these recent rustler raids. But it couldn't be true. Couldn't. . . .

Recalling Sheriff Crawford's stubborn attempt at fairness in the face of the antagonism of the others gave Joe Dorn a warm glow. He had unexpectedly found a friend this morning, his second in this country. Helen Norris was the other, although only instinct made him call her that. He seldom saw her, yet she had indefinably conveyed that impression that she wasn't with the others in disliking him. Crawford had been blunt, hard, but had demanded proof of what Bolt had sneeringly implied.

She didn't look so pleased with Bolt, either, Dorn told himself. Her tanned face had been pale with wordless anger as she had looked down at Bolt's limp figure, then she had smiled at Joe Dorn as though in apology for Bolt's action, thoroughly understanding.

That smile had disturbed him and even now set up within him strange currents of feeling. People said Helen Norris would someday marry Ren Bolt, but that one fleeting instant when her anger had unmasked her true feelings made Dorn doubt she loved Bolt.

At the top of the ridge he drew rein to rest his chestnut. From here he could see the buildings of his D Bar layout four miles away, backed by the first high crest of the foothills. For an instant he was filled with pride at what he and Morgan had done, then that shadow of doubt came clouding, and with it the necessity of knowing the truth.

Reckon I'll take my own sashay up the gulch, he mused as he swung his mount down off the lip of the rim, following the faint line of a trail that cut directly north. Then another thought came to him. *No use begging trouble. Crawford's posse will be on the move. Reckon I'll just cross over the pass and come in the back way.*

It was a long, hard ride over little traveled trails where fall rains had washed deep gullies and bared sharp rocks. He rode into snow higher up, a thin white blanket that weighed down the junipers and clung to the bare branches of the aspens.

Sundown found him across the high treeless pass and cutting east through the cedars along the far side of the peaks. He made his camp at dark, not trusting himself to find his way in this unfamiliar country. Somewhere, miles to the east, he would find the way into the head of Deep Gulch, and, if Sheriff Bob Crawford's guess was correct, he'd find the answer to the stolen herds of the Sawtooth range.

II

High noon of the following day Joe Dorn was pushing his way into the brush-choked upper end of a steep cañon. Ever since leaving the boulder fields, he had been cutting sign of a large herd; even the fall of new snow failed to hide it from his experienced eye. The brush here was broken-branched, proof enough for a greenhorn. And even though he reasoned that this cañon and its two-day-old trail would be deserted, he rode with his Winchester slanted across the saddle horn.

He came on it unexpectedly, at a point where the cañon had deepened so that its walls towered eighty feet above him. Showing between the fallen shards of a huge boulder was a flash of color that made the chestnut side-step and shy in nervousness. Dorn swiveled his rifle around with instant wariness. Then he saw the rigid hand reaching up out of the snow and the shape beneath the white blanket.

That splotch of color was a red bandanna—and the mound beneath the snow was Dan Morgan's body. As his rage suddenly gave way to deep bitterness, Dorn turned the body over and saw the torn, bloody hole in his friend's back. A shotgun hole. Both of Morgan's guns were sheathed, unfired.

He spent half an hour piling loose rock over the body, feeling that he had forever lost a vital part of himself. Then he unstrapped his gun belt, picked up Morgan's two belts out of the snow, the guns, two .45s, mates to the one he carried. He strapped them both on.

"Whatever the play was, deal me in, Dan," he breathed, his palms flat against the two holsters. "And I'll use your chips."

He was halfway out of Deep Gulch, headed for home, with the snow beginning to fall out of a dead gray sky, when he found Morgan's bay mare standing head down in the shelter of a cedar grove.

Joe Dorn took the trail to Sawtooth early the next morning. The eight-mile ride to the town, perched high on a rocky shelf backed by rimrock, took him two hours. He turned in at the tie rail in front of Edwards's Hardware Store.

He needed a few things—nails, a length of half-inch rope, a new pair of wire cutters; these could have waited but for the fact that Harry Edwards was the most talkative man in town and fairly friendly. And there was something he had to know before he went any further.

"Howdy, Dorn," Edwards greeted.

The store was deserted, and Dorn mumbled over the things he wanted.

The storekeeper noted his customer's gravity, and, believing he understood the reason for it, he said sympathetically: "That was an ornery trick Bolt played on you, Dorn. He won't make it stick."

Joe Dorn shrugged and made no answer.

"You know," Edwards went on, warming to his subject, "I don't believe that about Dan Morgan, either. He ain't the kind to take to vent brandin'. Hell, what'd they find? Not a damned thing but tracks and more tracks. They stayed out one night. Crawford wanted to go on over the pass the next mornin', but it looked like a storm comin' up and the boys backed out on him. Ren Bolt said they'd better throw a watch on your place and wait till Morgan come home, and save a lot of trouble and expense. Crawford shore give him a tongue-wallopin'."

"They're back, huh?" Joe Dorn queried idly. "How far did they go?"

"Only to the mouth of that cañon that spills into the gulch. That's as far as any posse's ever gone. If you ask me, I think some o' the boys had itchy spines . . . the kind a gent gits when he's expectin' a lead slug to tickle his backbone."

"Bolt in town today?" Joe Dorn asked.

The storekeeper nodded. "I seen his blue down at the corral."

Dorn paid for his purchases and sauntered out onto the street. The town was beginning to stir. A half dozen early risers were smoking on the hotel porch.

Now he was certain that the posse hadn't found Morgan's body. He went down the street to the sheriff's office in the adobe jail.

When he opened the door, Bert Welch was on his knees in

front of the stove, raking out the ashes below the fire he had just started. The deputy cast a glance at Joe Dorn, grunted, and went on with his task. Dorn took the chair behind the desk, and, when Welch straightened up, his eyes widened in astonishment.

"You figure to take over this office?" he asked in ill-concealed irritation. Plainly public opinion was bringing out his true feelings about Joe Dorn.

Calmly Dorn rolled a cigarette, answered only after lighting it.

"I thought maybe I'd find Crawford in. Supposing you go get him for me, Bert."

"You kin walk."

Dorn leaned back, regarding the deputy through narrowed lids. Finally he drawled: "You're one jasper I'm going to take apart one of these days, Bert. I'll make it any way you say. Guns, fists, knives . . . or rocks. But I'm forgetting my business. I'm here to make a deal with Crawford. I know where he can find Dan Morgan."

Bert Welch's angrily corded jaw muscles slackened and his mouth fell open.

"You know? You. . . ."

"I know where Morgan is. I'll be in town for two hours. If Crawford's interested in hearing about it, he'll find me over at the lunch room, getting a cup of coffee. I'm not making my deal with any understrapper, Bert."

The deputy forgot his belligerence in the face of this news. He reached for his Stetson and hurried to the door.

"I'll git Crawford," he jerked over his shoulder. "And don't you leave town."

Dorn watched the deputy going up the street. Welch's ponderous frame was moving faster than Dorn would have thought possible. Abreast the hotel, Welch hesitated, looking furtively back along the street. Joe Dorn grinned tightly, muttering: "Climb those steps, *hombre* . . . or make me a damned poor guesser."

Abruptly Bert Welch took the hotel steps two at a time and disappeared. Satisfied, Dorn left the sheriff's office, cut across the street, and entered the lunch room. When Bob Crawford found him there, he was finishing his second cup of coffee.

"Bert tells me you got some news, Dorn," the lawman said.

Joe Dorn nodded, threw a dime on the counter, and said: "Let's talk about it across the street."

When they were in the sheriff's office with the door closed and Bob Crawford had turned his puzzled gaze on his visitor, Dorn said: "Morgan is dead, Sheriff."

Crawford sat down heavily in his chair. "Then you trumped up a story for Bert. Why?"

"That'll come later. Dan Morgan is dead, Crawford."

"I'd give my left arm to have talked with him before he cashed in. I'm sorry to hear it, Dorn." Crawford was sincere.

"He couldn't've told you what you want to know," Dorn said, his voice flat-edged. "I found him yesterday in the cañon above the gulch, with a back full of buckshot. He'd been dead at least two days from his looks."

"Mebbe the wild bunch did it. Mebbe they had a reason."

Dorn shook his head. "Not the wild bunch you think. I'd bet my last dollar that Dan stumbled in there and found 'em driving that herd through."

Abruptly he broke off. He had been looking out the window up the street toward the hotel. He saw Ren Bolt come down the steps and stride hurriedly toward the jail.

"Give me a chance to prove what I think, Sheriff," he said quickly. "I've got an idea. You'll hear about it later. I told Bert Welch that trumped-up story so he'd tell it to Ren Bolt and get him down here. Bert thinks the sun rises and sets in Bolt.

There's Bolt across the street now, headed across here. When he comes in, you're going to hear some mighty queer things. Will you back me?"

Crawford's brown eyes were narrow-lidded as he regarded Joe Dorn. Finally he shrugged and said: "I've got nothing to lose."

When Ren Bolt stepped inside, Joe Dorn was saying: "So that's the deal I'll make you, Sheriff. Take it or leave it."

Bob Crawford was gazing down at his hands on the desk top before him, apparently so seriously considering Dorn's words that he appeared not to have heard Bolt enter.

"What's this I hear about Dan Morgan?" Bolt blurted.

Crawford glanced. "Who told you about it, Ren?"

"Welch." Bolt glanced at Dorn. "He says you know where we can find him, Dorn."

Dorn nodded and smiled thinly. "I've got him hidden," he drawled. "He came straying up to the ranch house last night with the back of his shirt cut to ribbons and bloody. Met up with a bushwhacker somewhere beyond the gulch. He can't talk much but from what I got out of him he must've run into the wild bunch the night they were driving their stolen beef through. He caught part of a charge of buckshot in his back. It didn't do the damage somebody thought, so he laid up there till they rode away, then managed to catch his bronc' and mosey on home. Took him two days to make the trip."

Ren Bolt's face gradually lost its ruddiness, took on a grayish tinge. Glancing briefly at Crawford, Dorn saw the lawman narrowly regarding Bolt, dawning suspicion in his eyes.

"That's a likely story," Ren Bolt growled. "We'd've cut his sign up there if what Dorn says is true."

"I've got to believe it," Crawford said. "Remember the snow that day, Ren? Remember we didn't go above the gulch? If we had, we'd've run onto Dan. Now I reckon we've got to do what

Dorn says." The lawman put the lie levelly, instinctively realizing that Joe Dorn had been right in framing this story to test Ren Bolt.

"And what does Dorn want us to do?"

"I've told Crawford I'd blindfold him and take him to see Dan," Dorn said reluctantly. "Not today, because Dan can't talk yet. Maybe tomorrow, or the next day. Maybe Dan saw something up the gulch that would interest a lawman."

Bolt's arrogance returned. "Morgan will lie. Crawford, any forked jasper will lie to save his hide. Why don't you round up a posse and look for him yourself? Arrest Dorn and keep him here until you've got the straight of this."

"I'll run this office the way I want, Bolt," the lawman flared. "If I figure Dorn's talking straight, I'll go wherever he takes me."

Angrily the rancher turned on his heel and stalked to the door, pausing for a parting jibe. "Sooner or later the law will catch up with you two, Dorn. If it don't, mebbe I'll take a hand."

"Any time," Dorn drawled. "Any time, *hombre.*"

After the door had closed behind Bolt, Crawford eyed Dorn speculatively. At length he said: "You wanted Ren to believe Morgan was alive. Why?"

Dorn got up from his chair and went to the window.

"Let's watch him," he said mysteriously.

They watched Ren Bolt as he went toward the hotel. But two doors short of it he turned in through the swing doors of a saloon. Crawford shrugged.

"All right. Let me in on it, Joe."

"Keep your eye on that saloon," Dorn told him shortly.

Puzzled, the lawman stood in silence for two minutes. Then they saw a man leave the saloon, go the tie rail out front, and climb onto a rangy bay gelding.

"Take a good look at that ranny," Dorn said grimly. "Red

flannel shirt, gray Stetson, black-handled irons, sheepskin coat. Watch him slope out of town, Sheriff."

The rider wheeled his bay and trotted past the jail. Once beyond it, he bent low in the saddle and put the animal into a fast lope.

"The word's on its way," Dorn said, grimness edging his voice.

"What word?" Crawford was plainly at a loss.

"Ren Bolt is sending that rider up the gulch with the news that Dan Morgan is still alive."

III

It was as if someone had hit Sheriff Crawford between the eyes. His fists bunched, then opened, as he rubbed his palms along the butts of his guns.

"It's time for straight talk, Dorn," he snapped. "You're accusing Ren Bolt of being too interested in what happened to Morgan?"

"It's a guess, Sheriff. I know a few things you don't, that's all. First, Morgan had money, plenty of it. Next, Bolt has always wanted to own our outfit. This might be his way of getting us plumb out of his way. I can't tell you why Dan was up the gulch that night, but I'm laying my chips against his knowing a thing about swinging a sticky loop. He wasn't that kind."

The lawman sat down heavily, eyes staring vacantly at the opposite wall. "I'd've said the same thing about Dan Morgan," he said slowly. "But every sign pointed the other way."

"Sure," Dorn agreed. "It was framed that way." He hesitated, then said sharply: "I'm headed for the hills, Sheriff. Maybe the gent that just left town'll lead me to something we'd all like to know."

Crawford stood up, the line of his shelving jaw blunt.

"I'm ridin' with you, Dorn," he snapped. "Give me time to

let Bert know where I'm headed."

"Forget Welch. He went straight to Ren Bolt when he was supposed to be getting you down here, didn't he?"

"Say that again."

Joe Dorn shook his head. "I don't know a thing for sure. But we ought to be careful. Ride out of here without telling a soul where you're headed. Let me leave ten minutes ahead of you. There's plenty of time . . . I know a short cut to the mouth of the gulch."

The sheriff nodded, a look of admiration creeping into his eyes.

"Mebbe I won't be sorry I called that pack of hounds off you the other day. Mebbe I was right, after all."

Dorn had reached for the door when it suddenly swung open. A girl stood framed in the opening; she was small and had a pretty face, but her two bright green eyes were red-rimmed, as if she had been crying.

"I wanted to see the sheriff," she said, forcing a worried smile.

She didn't move from the doorway, so Dorn was compelled to stay where he was, to listen to what she had to say.

"I'm from Rock Crossing, beyond the mountains," she said hastily. "I . . . I came in a few minutes ago on the stage, looking for a man. Maybe you can help me." She appeared not to be conscious of Joe Dorn's presence.

"I'd be glad to oblige," the lawman told her. "Who was he?"

"He . . . he was to have ridden over from here day before yesterday," she said haltingly. "He and I were to be married. I'm worried because he didn't come." She dabbed at her eyes, then her head went up and she went on bravely: "He wouldn't do a thing like that . . . unless something had happened. Never!"

"Tell me his name," the sheriff said levelly, and with startling suddenness Joe Dorn knew what he was thinking even before the girl spoke.

"Dan Morgan. Can you help me find him?"

Both men stood stunned, until the alarm in the girl's eyes made Dorn say, in a lighter tone than he thought he could command: "I wouldn't worry about Dan. He'll show up. So you're the girl he's been riding out to see every month or so? He never told us."

The girl's smile was still fearful. "Yes. Dan came to see me whenever he could get away. He . . . we thought we'd keep it a secret until he could bring me home with him."

Crawford sighed, looking to Joe Dorn for help.

"Why don't you put up at the hotel until we have a chance to ride out and see Dan," Dorn asked the girl. "There's nothing to worry about, Miss . . . ?"

"Moira Grant," she said.

"That's what you'd better do, Miss Grant," Crawford put in. "It won't take us long."

"Thank you," the girl said simply.

She turned and went out the door, closing it after her. Dorn and Crawford went to the window and watched her cross the street to the hotel and go up the steps.

"That about settles it," Sheriff Crawford muttered. "So there's where Dan Morgan was doing his rustling . . . across the hills in Rock Crossing. How're we going to tell her, Dorn?"

That had been troubling Dorn for the last five minutes. In a way, the duty was his own, since he was Morgan's friend, but telling a woman a thing like this was something he just couldn't do. Abruptly he had an idea.

"We might stop and see Helen Norris on the way out to the gulch. She could come into town and take care of the girl, and do a better job of breaking the news than either of us."

When they reached the Split Diamond, the sheriff did the talking. Helen Norris and her father sat before the big fieldstone fireplace, listening. As the lawman told John Norris and his daughter what he suspected, what he had discovered, the girl's glance swung around to Joe Dorn.

At first a white-hot, accusing anger flared into her hazel eyes as she heard the sheriff's suspicions of Ren Bolt. But as he gave her proof, Dorn knew, when she looked at him, that she had been deeply hurt.

Her head held proudly high, she said quietly: "I believe you honestly think Ren is in back of all this, Sheriff Crawford. I don't. But I'll go in and take care of the girl." She got quickly up and left the room.

"It's hard on her," John Norris said. "It's hard on me, too. We both think a lot of Ren. I'm shore hopin' you're wrong about him, Bob."

"It hit me hard as it's hitting you," Crawford told the rancher. "But I can't overlook facts."

When he and Joe Dorn left a few minutes later, a cowpuncher down at the corral was leading out a team of roans toward the buckboard. Helen Norris was leaving for town, to break the news to the girl Dan Morgan had chosen for his wife.

"We'll have to ride," Crawford said, scanning the trail ahead.

"Let's let that gent up ahead get into the gulch before we do," Dorn suggested. "There's snow up there and we can cut his sign."

For two hours they held their ponies to a mile-eating trot. Then they cut into the hills in a roundabout way toward Deep Gulch. Noon saw them swinging into the rocky mouth of the gulch where the high walls cut out all sunlight but a broad ribbon high above.

They were climbing continually. After their noonday halt for a meal they rode out the head of the gulch and into the higher, broader cañon. There was snow here, and fresh sign.

"He's ahead of us," Crawford drawled. "Mebbe we ought to go faster."

But Dorn quickly changed the lawman's idea. "We maybe got twenty more miles to ride," he said. "I've thought for a long time that this bunch must have an outlet the other side of the mountains, a ranch, a rail spur, some way of getting rid of the critters they steal. We've got plenty of time, Sheriff."

His prediction was correct, for at sundown they were still following that plainly marked sign of a single rider. It was taking them above timberline, heading straight for a low pass between the peaks that towered above them. When they gained the windswept boulder fields shortly after dusk, the snow gave out.

"We'll eat and go on," the lawman said, plainly impatient. "There'll be a moon later, and more snow on the other side. I'd like to pick up this *hombre*'s sign again and follow it in the dark. We're two damned good targets in the daylight."

So they backtracked until they reached a growth of scrub oak to make their fire in the lee of a low outcropping and cook their meal. It was shortly before midnight, after they had gone on through the pass and down the smooth far side in the light of a cold quarter moon, that they picked up sign again. And then, as they were dropping into a narrow cañon, the sharp *crack* of a Winchester slapped out across the night.

As the echo beat down the cañon, they spurred toward an aspen grove. Sheriff Crawford groaned faintly and went loose in the saddle. Dorn saw him clutch at the saddle horn and finally straighten, muttering a curse.

"Damn!" the oldster rasped, looking sharply above and ahead. "Busted my arm, I guess. You better have a look, pardner."

Dorn swung out of his saddle, drawing his rifle from its scabbard. Cautiously, his gaze focused on the high wall, he stepped back to Crawford's pony and helped the lawman climb down. As Crawford sat down, he knelt beside the sheriff, took off his sheepskin, and tore away the sleeve from the injured arm. But he kept an anxious eye on that spot high on the opposite wall of the cañon.

"You called it, Sheriff," he said glumly. "It's a bad break."

Quickly he stopped the flow of blood from the wound with his bandanna, made a splint of a green aspen branch, and bound it about the arm. Then, picking up his rifle, he said tersely: "Stay here, and I'll have a try at that coyote up there."

Twenty yards below Crawford and the horses, he stopped, listening for a sound that would give away the position of the hidden gunman. But all he heard was the sighing of the wind through the branches of the leafless aspens, and far below the haunting night cry of a coyote, howling at the moon.

Carefully he lined the sights of his rifle at the point from which the mushroom of powder light had come. He levered two quick shots, then changed his position before the echoes of the gun thunder had died out.

There was an instant answer. Three shots winked out from high above. And Joe Dorn met the third sharp report of that hidden gun with an answering shot. Until his weapon's hammer *clicked* on an empty chamber, he sent bullets flying toward the bushwhacker's hiding spot, setting up a deafening inferno of sound in the narrow cañon.

Once he thought he heard a cry above the gun echoes. But no answer came to his last burst of shots. Then, from across the cañon, he heard rocks falling, a dull thud and a breaking of branches, as though some weighty object had fallen through the tree tops.

He waited five minutes longer, but there was no further sound. Going back to Crawford, he found the lawman sitting, tight-lipped and pale, holding his injured arm. But when Crawford saw Dorn, he let go of his arm and pointed across the cañon.

"You'll find him over there, Dorn," he said tightly. "At the foot of that tallest aspen. That was damned good sighting."

And it had been, with Dorn's only target the winking gun flash of those answering shots.

Circling wide of the trees, he crossed the cañon floor. In two minutes he was standing above a sprawled figure in the snow. His lips tightened as he recognized the dead man as the rider he had seen leave the saloon in such a hurry that morning. He pulled the body back into the darkness of the aspen grove and went back to the sheriff.

"Then he didn't get to 'em with his news yet," Crawford said, when Dorn told him who the dead man was. A deep frown furrowed the lawman's brow. "We're out of luck, Dorn. From here on it's guesswork. We're riding blind."

"I'm riding blind. You're heading back to town to get that arm looked after."

Crawford shook his head. "And let you walk into this alone," he snorted. "Nope. This is my job, Dorn."

Joe argued against the sheriff's stubbornness and it was only after telling Crawford that he'd be in the way, wounded as he was, that this was a one-man job from here on, that the lawman gave in.

"You get that arm fixed and wait for me," Dorn insisted firmly. "I won't go into anything I can't finish. All I want is to find out where they're hiding the stolen beef and spot their hide-out. After that a posse can handle things."

The lawman waited while he followed the dead man's sign to the point where he had climbed from his saddle and started up the wall. There he found the bay horse the man had ridden out of town that morning. Quickly changing saddles and bridles, he took his chestnut back to Crawford.

"Take my bronc' back over the pass with you," he said. "You can turn him loose up there and he'll find his way home. I'm straddling our friend's jughead. It'll maybe come in handy."

IV

Sheriff Crawford, his arm strapped tightly across his chest, took the back trail. His face was drawn with pain and it was plain he'd have a hard ride back to town. But Joe Dorn knew the man. Sheriff Bob Crawford had plenty of grit. He'd make the ride safely.

Dorn waited until the lawman, leading the chestnut, had climbed out of sight a quarter of a mile above. Then he rode on in the opposite direction, feeling out the unfamiliar gait of the bay. He was satisfied after the first two hundred yards.

He had ridden three miles when trouble descended without warning. A voice bellowed out from the trees: "Shove up your hands, *hombre!*"

Dorn dropped his reins and raised his hands to the level of his ears. He heard the muffled hoofs of a walking horse close by, then he saw a moving shadow among the trees—a rider with a rifle slanted across his chest.

The man drew rein twenty feet away, settling his stocky body at a slouch in his saddle.

"Lookin' for somethin'?" he drawled.

"Cattle," Dorn said with a forced grin. "Bolt sent me up with news."

In the pale snow-reflected light of the moon, he saw the man's eyes squint, then smear over inscrutably. "Who's Bolt?"

"A twelve-hour ride and I've got to set here while you ask me damn' fool questions," Dorn growled. "Ren sent me up with news, I tell you."

The rider's expression changed to a shade of uncertainty. "*Hombre,* I never seen you before. How I know you ain't runnin' a sandy?"

"You heard those shots up above, didn't you?"

The man nodded briefly. "That's why I'm up here. Sounded like a plumb army."

Dorn shrugged. "Just three jaspers with more curiosity than sense trailing me across the pass. I forted up in the rocks and persuaded 'em to turn around. One of their jugheads was carrying double when they left."

The rider's eye was running over the bay Dorn rode.

"That's Pete's bay," he said abruptly.

Dorn nodded. "My roan picked up a stone bruise coming in yesterday. Bolt told me to take Pete's, since I was a stranger and he wanted a way of your knowing me. He didn't bring me in on this to sit out in the cold with my hands and feet going numb, answering a lot of fancy talk, either. Let's get going. I need a cup of coffee . . . hot."

"I'll take you on in," the man said, but his voice still held a trace of his wariness. "Only shuck your irons and let me carry 'em for you."

Dorn slowly shook his head, lowering his hands and folding them on the saddle horn. "No, you don't. I like to have my plow handles handy."

The rider hesitated, then abruptly lifted his shoulders in a shrug, and thrust his Winchester into the boot beneath his saddle.

"All right," he said curtly.

He whistled sharply and from across the cañon two riders sloped out of the shelter of the trees and came toward them.

"A new man Ren sent up," the rider who had accosted Joe Dorn announced when they drew rein. He shot a glance at Dorn. "What's the news you brought us, pardner?"

"Ren said for me only to give it to the boss."

For a long moment the three eyed him coldly. Then one of the other two riders said: "That's not like Ren. We're all in on this."

Dorn shrugged casually. "I'm being paid to follow orders."

His words were final, although he could see that two of the

men were on the point of retorting hotly. But their words were cut off as the third rider, a tall, gaunt man with a vicious face, laughed coldly and drawled: "This is somethin' new. Let's do like he says and take him to see Polter."

Helen Norris had driven into town late that morning, alone. She was tying the buckboard team to the hitch rail in front of the hotel when Ren Bolt sauntered down the steps toward her, with a smile on his darkly handsome face.

"Hello, Helen. What's bringin' you in?"

There was something Helen Norris had to find out at once for her own peace of mind. She had never loved Ren Bolt, but he was her father's choice and therefore hers. She had accepted him, determined to overlook his arrogance, his greed for money and land, hoping that someday she might learn to love him.

But the suspicion Sheriff Crawford and Joe Dorn had planted in her mind had to be settled here and now. And forgetting that the safety of Joe Dorn and the sheriff might depend on her, she said impetuously: "Ren, I want the truth. Did you have Dan Morgan killed?"

His eyes sharpened into wariness, but the girl did not notice that.

"Did I have Morgan killed?" he echoed, his smile broadening disarmingly. "Why should I? What makes you ask?"

"I want an answer," she retorted hotly. "The girl Morgan was going to marry is waiting for me in there . . . waiting to hear that he's dead!"

"Dead?" Bolt's look hardened. "Who told you that?"

She caught herself then, realized suddenly how much she'd been on the verge of telling Ren Bolt.

But he stepped close to her, took her arm in a hard grip as he rasped: "Who told you Dan Morgan was dead?"

She jerked her arm away, wincing from the tight grip. Here

was proof enough to her, and the realization of it made her strangely happy. And oddly enough her thoughts flew to Joe Dorn, as she swiftly decided she must do something to remove the suspicion she'd planted in Ren Bolt's mind.

"No one told me he was dead," she lied calmly. Then, looking him squarely in the eye: "You forget yourself, Ren."

He stepped back in embarrassment, reddening at the realization of having shown her a side of him she didn't know.

"I'm sorry," he apologized humbly. "Only this blamed thing has me on edge."

"Why should it?" she queried very sharply.

He shifted his thick shoulders nervously and his ruddy face took on a still deeper tide of color. "It's . . . well, it's because of what I said the other day, what I know is true. Dan Morgan was a rustler."

"Was?"

He was angry now, his eyes blazing as he sought to hide his emotion. He was groping for an answer as Helen whirled and left him. As she disappeared through the hotel doorway, a heavy frown blackened his face, and he was no longer handsome. Abruptly he turned and headed for the jail.

Bert Welch was in the sheriff's office dozing, with his feet on the desk.

Ren Bolt shook the deputy into wakefulness.

"Where's Crawford?" he asked gruffly as soon as Welch was wide-awake.

"He rode out to Ray Temple's . . . to look the place over."

"Temple's? Are you shore?"

Welch nodded, but as he saw the glint of hardness in Bolt's eyes, he asked anxiously: "Is somethin' wrong, Ren?"

Spacing his words evenly, the big rancher said: "Helen Norris jest told me Dan Morgan is dead. She didn't realize what she'd said till too late. She knows somethin'."

"What does she know?" Welch snapped, fear in his eyes now.

"I don't know. But it's somethin'. It means we've played plumb into their hands, sendin' Pete up to the hide-out."

"Whose hands?" Welch's face was sallow-looking.

"Crawford's," Bolt snarled. "And that damn' Joe Dorn's."

"I swear to God I didn't cross you." Bert Welch shrank down into his chair. "But, listen, Ren, I want to git outta this. I don't want to be mixed up in it. The only thing I ever done was to fake the tally on them beef shipments. I'll never breathe a word, Ren, but count me out."

Bolt's smile was evil as he focused a hard glance on the deputy.

"You couldn't buy out with twice the money I paid you, Bert," he said silkily. "No, not with ten times as much. Because right now you're forkin' that jughead of yours and comin' with me to the hide-out. I've a hunch I kin use you."

The deputy's face was a sickly gray. Twice he opened his mouth to speak; each time words failed to come. At length he nodded dumbly, got up from his chair, and started toward the door.

"I'd hate to have you sidin' Dan Morgan," Bolt said meaningfully, following the deputy. "Play this my way, Bert, and pretty soon we'll all be in the clear."

The trail led down out of the cañon and into a broad valley that was hemmed in on three sides by rimrock. Half a mile back, Joe Dorn and the three men who rode with him had been challenged by a guard stationed high on the cañon wall.

Here Dorn could see far enough by the light of the moon to realize that Ren Bolt had chosen a perfect spot for his work. Scattered bunches of a large herd dotted the broad sweep of the valley, for here the grass was still green and would probably be good most of the winter, sheltered as it was from the winds of the mountain slope. Far across the valley, a light winked out against the darkness, indicating the location of a cabin.

The three riders who rode with Dorn had accepted his statement that Ren Bolt had sent him here. And now that he was here, he was seeing proof of what had before been a conviction—although a firm one. Several hundred head of prime steers had disappeared from the Sawtooth range in the past year, building up the rustler accusation that Ren Bolt had planned saddling on Dan Morgan.

Dorn could see the whole thing clearly now as his lips tightened at the realization of how Ren Bolt had planned to name Morgan and Joe Dorn as rustlers. And the carefully laid scheme had already halfway carried.

Shortly the four riders were dismounting in the littered yard before a small slab shack. A man came out of the shadows and led the horses toward the corral that stood outlined below the shack.

Looking out across the valley again, picking out the deep mouth of the cañon that spilled into it, Dorn commented appreciatively: "Nice layout you've got here."

"Yeah, shore," one of the trio agreed. "Good grass, water, and all the time we need."

"Which way do you drive the stuff when the brands are healed?" Dorn queried. That was the last thing he had to know.

"Back the way they come," was the laconic answer. "Down Deep Gulch and onto King Bolt range."

There it was—a flawless way for Ren's King Bolt to swallow these vanished herds. But Joe Dorn certainly meant to check up on the King Bolt's roundup count the next time he had the chance.

The shack was a single room, bunks at one end, a slab table and benches in the center opposite the door, and a squat hogback stove at the far end with a rack of pans and a stack of canned goods behind it.

A lamp burned at the table's center, and beyond it, sitting in the shadow, was the outline of a man.

"What was it?" the shadowed man demanded.

The gaunt man with the skull-like countenance answered: "Bolt sent a new man in with news, Polter. He wanted to see you before he spilled it."

The man called Polter stood up, stepped into the light. He was short, thin, yet his eyes gave a hint as to why he was the leader. They were a muddy blue, hard, and somehow made a man glance to see how he wore his guns and to look at his thin, tapering hands.

"Well?" he queried again, his voice metallic. His eyes were boring into Joe Dorn.

"Bolt got the news yesterday morning that Dan Morgan showed up at his layout alive," Joe Dorn announced.

The cloudy light left Polter's eyes. They took on brightness.

"Whoever said that lied," he said flatly. "Ren Bolt hisself planted a double charge o' buckshot square in that *hombre*'s back. Bolt don't miss. I saw it."

Dorn shrugged. "I'm not claiming it's true, but Joe Dorn, Morgan's pardner, brought that story in to the sheriff. He claimed he could take the sheriff to see Dan Morgan, claimed he had him hidden, and that he was shot up bad but alive."

Polter betrayed no emotion. His face was inscrutable, his eyes cloudy once more.

"We better throw a guard around here," he said. "Morgan couldn't be alive and whoever says so is startin' a play against us. Anyone follow you in, *hombre?*"

"Three jaspers I smoked out at the head of the cañon."

"Yeah, that's what all the shootin' was about," the gaunt man put in.

"You let 'em git away, Slim?" Polter snarled, eyeing the gaunt man.

Slim shrugged. "This gent here. . . ."

"The handle's Mace . . . Jack Mace." Dorn supplied the first name that came to him.

"Mace, here," Slim went on, "says he winged one of the three and sent 'em back up the cañon. We didn't follow, thinkin' it was more important to bring Mace in. Red's standin' look-out."

"Then there's nothin' to stop anybody from ridin' in as far as the look-out!" Polter blazed. "Slim, you are a damn' fool! So are you, Spence, and you, Harry!" He cursed and went on derisively: "We're bein' paid plenty to swing our end of this without a hitch. And you three leave the gates open to the first proddy jasper that wants to come in and spot us!"

Joe Dorn heard the door open behind him, heard a familiar drawl: "Turn around, Dorn."

It was Ren Bolt's voice.

V

The words died out in the sudden silence before Joe Dorn followed his instinct. Slim, beside him, was facing the door as Joe Dorn wheeled behind the tall man, his hands streaking to his guns. He kicked out stiffly with one booted foot and sent the heavy table crashing to the floor. A gun blast lighted the room as the lamp guttered out, and Dorn felt Slim's body jerk spasmodically. Slim coughed and sank to the floor. Bolt had killed his own man in a try for Joe Dorn.

In the darkness Dorn knelt on the floor to one side of Slim, waiting, trying to pick up some sound that would betray Bolt's presence. Then Bolt's voice spoke out of the silence far to one side of him.

"I'm over here, Polter, behind the stove. It's Joe Dorn you brought in here, Dan Morgan's pardner. He's not to git out alive! He's in the center of the room! Let's blast him out!"

"Hold on!" Polter called that sharp command from somewhere behind Joe along the wall. "You hit Slim when you made that try for Dorn! We'll be cuttin' each other to doll rags if we open up like this! You can't do it!"

Swiftly Dorn thumbed two shots in the direction of Polter's voice. The walls beat back an inferno of sound as the scene was feebly lighted for a split second. Polter was too wise to answer Dorn's fire and give away his hiding place, but blasting gun flashes flared out from behind the stove and Dorn felt the air rush of the bullets as they sped by the spot where his own gun had flashed. But he had dodged silently aside.

On the heels of Bolt's third shot came a soughing grunt from the room's far end. A choked cry sounded, Spence's voice. "Damn you, Bolt! A busted shoulder!"

Joe thumbed back the hammer of his gun and let it fall in a shot aimed at Spence. As the thunder of the explosion faded, he heard the thud of a body hitting the floor.

"Spence!" Ren Bolt called, but there was no answer. Spence was dead.

Silently Dorn worked his way to the back wall and inched his way along it, hoping to gain the cover of the heavy slab table. Suddenly his foot struck something that moved, and the next instant a blow hit him on his left shoulder. He had blundered into Polter in the darkness, and the man's downswinging gun had clubbed him.

Wincing from the pain of that blow, he swiveled up the snout of gun and squeezed the trigger. In the powder flame of that upward shot he saw Polter's twisted face dimly outlined, and his next bullet centered the rustler chief's forehead.

Polter fell on him in a loose sprawl that pinned him so that he couldn't move for a second or two. And in that interval two shots roared out from Ren Bolt's hidden position. Dorn felt the whip of the slugs as they tore into Polter's lifeless body.

"You all right, Polter?" Bolt yelled.

A heavy silence was his only answer. It lasted for a full half minute, as beads of perspiration dampened Joe Dorn's forehead. It had been close. He would have been dead but for Polter's bulk.

Suddenly there was panic in Ren Bolt's voice as he bawled: "Spence! Slim! Polter! Answer me, damn it! Where are you?"

"Losin' your nerve?" drawled the voice of Bolt's only remaining gunman, Harry. He was over near the door, and Dorn heard the hinges of the panel grate softly as it swung open. "I'm leavin' you, Ren. You've built your own fight . . . now let's see you finish it!"

The rustler's shape was outlined for a flashing instant in the lighter shadow of the doorway, and in that spit second Ren Bolt's gun spoke again, not at Joe Dorn, but at the fleeing shadow of his own man.

Dorn saw Harry's stride break, lag, and then the man's thick bulk was falling forward into the shadows outside.

Dorn could hear Ren Bolt's heavy breathing and muttered a curse.

Abruptly Bolt called out in a loud voice: "Bert! Are you outside, Bert?"

Almost as his answer came the hoof pound of a fast-ridden horse. As it faded out in the night's stillness, Joe Dorn, behind the shelter of the table, drawled: "You're alone now, Bolt. So Bert Welch rode up with you, did he? I never did trust him. But you won't see him again."

"Come and git me, Dorn!" Bolt shouted.

"I will," was Joe Dorn's ominous promise.

He had just discovered something that set his pulses leaping. He had not forgotten that Red, the guard on lookout at the mouth of the cañon, was probably riding hell-bent right now to take a hand in the fight. And with Red outside to help Bolt, Joe Dorn's chances looked pretty slim.

Or they had until his hand had touched something cold on the floor and he had discovered it to be the lamp base, unbroken as the chimney had been, and half full of kerosene.

He could still hear Ren Bolt's heavy breathing. He tried to picture that end of the room, tried to place exactly the broad front of the heavy cast-iron stove. Bolt would be behind it, protected by those heavy iron plates.

The picture came clear. At the back wall there had been a crate of canned goods. Alongside that stood a squat water barrel with a two-foot space between it and the stove. The most important thing was his remembering the warmth that had drifted out into the room from the stove. Even though the cabin door now stood open, letting in a blast of chill air, he could feel that warmth. There would be live coals in the stove.

Slowly, soundlessly he came to his knees. The darkness was complete, so that he had to reach out and feel of the table's rim to be sure he cleared it. Then, drawing back his arm, and with the lamp base held tightly in his hand, he hurled it toward the stove.

There was a long, split second's wait until he heard the *crash*. He dropped behind the shelter of the table once more as Ren Bolt shouted a startled oath. He waited for what seemed an eternity, yet it was for the space of only three seconds.

Suddenly there was the sound of bursting flames and a bright orange light wiped out the shadows. Dorn surged up from behind the table, his two guns swiveling up. He saw Ren Bolt stagger out from behind the stove with his shirt ablaze. Bolt's face was twisted in agony, yet he made no attempt to beat out the blazing shirt; instead, he stood, spraddle-legged, with his gun lined and shot first.

Dorn felt the bullet whip into his right shoulder, saw instantly that his answering shot had gone wide of its mark. He steadied the gun, drew back the hammer, and met Ren Bolt's second gun blast with one of his own. Again he felt the solid impact of a lead slug as it ricocheted from the table corner and seared a burn along his left side. But Ren Bolt's massive body had jerked in a pain spasm on the heel of his shot and his right arm fell lifelessly to his side.

A blinding rage took hold of Joe Dorn then. Here was Dan Morgan's killer, a man who was the killer of two of his own men. A cold, calculating accuracy aimed Dorn's guns. He thumbed them empty at Bolt's tottering bulk, a deathly grin on his face as he saw the bullets drive the man back to the wall.

Bolt was dead before his knees gave way, his broad chest a bloody mass. He fell against the blazing stove, with his boots already seared from the heat of the tinder-dry, flaming end wall.

Joe Dorn felt weakness hit him, a weariness that made him want to close his eyes. He took a step and a stabbing pain in his side cleared his senses. He reached up with his left hand, ran it along his side, and brought it away bloody. And to add to the torment of that searing pain, he felt a duller throb in his right shoulder.

Hazily, knowing only that he must leave the burning cabin, he staggered to the door. He had forgotten his guns and remembered them only as the night's chill struck him like a tonic.

He returned, looked back, and saw his guns lying alongside the overturned table—not his guns, but Dan Morgan's.

"You won that deal, Morg," he muttered.

Then a sudden wave of weakness hit him and he stumbled out to drop dazedly to the ground and sit there, staring dully at the blaze as it began to lick up the outside of the shack's wall.

Sheriff Bob Crawford rode up on his lathered horse. The blaze was high now; the blaze the sheriff had seen from the far end of the valley. The lawman's jaw was set grimly, not so much from the pain of his broken arm as from what he had done a few minutes before.

More than an hour ago, above near the pass, he had heard riders coming toward him. He had ridden to one side of the trail and hidden in a growth of stunted cedars—and seen Ren Bolt ride past with Bert Welch. He had known of Welch's betrayal then, had guessed how the deputy had made it possible for Bolt to get rid of the stolen herds.

So the sheriff had turned quickly back to follow Bolt and Bert Welch toward the hide-out. Bolt and Welch had ridden too far ahead of him for him to be near them when they reached the shack, but he had met Bert Welch as he raced back up the cañon, fleeing from the gun thunder behind him.

Crawford had reined up in front of Welch, had seen the fear that surged into his deputy's eyes. They had drawn their guns together—but it was Welch who was dead.

The sheriff found Joe Dorn just sitting there, unmindful of the blistering heat that swept out at him, a dull, unblinking stare in his eyes. He lifted Dorn to his feet and led him down the slope. He made him lie down, then ran over to the stream that flowed close in to the foot of the knoll. He came back and threw a hatful of water in Dorn's face and was relieved to see the look of surprise that brightened the young rancher's eyes.

Dorn weakly raised a hand and wiped the water from his face, grinning feebly. "I thought I sent you home," he said.

Before Crawford could answer, there came the sound of distant hoof thunder.

"More of this crew?" the lawman snapped.

Quickly he helped Joe Dorn to his feet and led him back into the shelter of a thicket. There they waited, Sheriff Crawford holding a six-gun in his left hand.

Half a dozen horsemen pounded in out of the shadows. There was a shout, and the lawman breathed a sigh of relief.

"That you, Norris?" he yelled.

Then Joe Dorn recognized the Split Diamond brand on the jaw of the nearest pony. He made out John Norris's portly bulk in the half light of the blaze. Then he heard Helen Norris ask Crawford, her voice giving way her alarm: "What happened to Joe?"

"He's over here," Crawford told her. "He's shot up a little. Wait and I'll take you to. . . ."

But she was already out of her saddle and running toward Dorn. He staggered up and stood uncertainly on his feet. She stopped a few feet from him, seeing his bloody shoulder and side.

"You're alive, Joe?" she murmured. "What happened to Ren?"

For a moment the tide of feeling that lay in her tones awed him. Finally he nodded toward the burning shack.

"He's in there," he said briefly.

With a choked cry she came up to him, looking into his face.

"It was my fault, Joe," she said penitently. "My fault that Ren came up here. I told him about Dan being dead. I had to know . . . about Ren. When I saw him leave town, I knew where he was going. I got Dad and these others, praying we'd be in time." She paused, and the look he read in her eyes wiped away the pain of his shoulder and his bleeding side. "I'm sorry, Joe. So terribly sorry."

His lean face took on a sober look. "Maybe it's my turn to be sorry. I shot up the man you picked for a husband."

She shook her head and smiled. "No, Joe. Ren shot up the man I picked. But he's going to get well." And as his eyes widened in disbelief, she stood on tiptoe and kissed him.

ACKNOWLEDGMENTS

"Outcast Deputy" first appeared as "Land-Grabber, I'll Be Back with Guns" in *Complete Western Book Magazine* (3/41). Copyright © 1941 by Newsstand Publications, Inc. Copyright © renewed 1969 by Dorothy S. Ewing. Copyright © 2008 by Dorothy S. Ewing for restored material.

"The Bullet" first appeared as "Dead Man's Sixes" in *Fifteen Western Tales* (9/48). Copyright © 1948 by Popular Publications, Inc. Copyright © renewed 1976 by Dorothy S. Ewing. Copyright © 2008 by Dorothy S. Ewing for restored material.

"Doc Gentry" first appeared as "A Button Sides a Saw-Bones" in *Ace-High Magazine* (6/37). Copyright © 1937 by Popular Publications, Inc. Copyright © renewed 1965 by Dorothy S. Ewing. Copyright © 2008 by Dorothy S. Ewing for restored material.

"A Notch for Bill Dagley" first appeared as "The Cowman They Couldn't Kill" in *10 Story Western* (8/37). Copyright © 1937 by Popular Publications, Inc. Copyright © renewed 1965 by Dorothy S. Ewing. Copyright © 2008 by Dorothy S. Ewing for restored material.

"Stone Walls" first appeared as "Stone Walls Make a Town-Tamer" in *Dime Western* (9/37). Copyright © 1937 by Popular

ABOUT THE AUTHOR

Peter Dawson is the *nom de plume* used by Jonathan Hurff Glidden. He was born in Kewanee, Illinois, and was graduated from the University of Illinois with a degree in English literature. In his career as a Western writer he published sixteen Western novels and wrote over 120 Western short novels and short stories for the magazine market. From the beginning he was a dedicated craftsman who revised and polished his fiction until it shone as a fine gem. His Peter Dawson novels are noted for their adept plotting, interesting and well-developed characters, their authentically researched historical backgrounds, and his stylistic flair. During the Second World War, Glidden served with the U.S. Strategic and Tactical Air Force in the United Kingdom. Later in 1950 he served for a time as Assistant to Chief of Station in Germany. After the war, his novels were frequently serialized in *The Saturday Evening Post.* Peter Dawson titles such as *Royal Gorge* and *Ruler of the Range* are generally conceded to be among his best titles, although he was an extremely consistent writer, and virtually all his fiction has retained its classic stature among readers of all generations. One of Jon Glidden's finest techniques was his ability, after the fashion of Dickens and Tolstoy, to tell his stories via a series of dramatic vignettes which focus on a wide assortment of different characters, all tending to develop their own lives, situations, and predicaments, while at the same time propelling the general plot of the story toward a suspenseful conclusion. He was no less gifted as a master of the short novel and short story. *Dark Riders of Doom* (Five Star Westerns, 1996) was the first collection of his Western short novels and stories to be published. His next Five Star Western will be *Gunsmoke Masquerade.*